# Legacy Fallen

# Legacy Fallen

Steven M. Chaplin Jr.

Copyright © 2011 by Steven M. Chaplin Jr.

Library of Congress Control Number:   2011915197
ISBN:          Hardcover         978-1-4653-5648-2
               Softcover         978-1-4653-5647-5
               Ebook             978-1-4653-5649-9

All rights reserved. No part of this book may be reproduced or transmitted in any form or by any means, electronic or mechanical, including photocopying, recording, or by any information storage and retrieval system, without permission in writing from the copyright owner.

This is a work of fiction. Names, characters, places and incidents either are the product of the author's imagination or are used fictitiously, and any resemblance to any actual persons, living or dead, events, or locales is entirely coincidental.

This book was printed in the United States of America.

To order additional copies of this book, contact:
Xlibris Corporation
1-888-795-4274
www.Xlibris.com
Orders@Xlibris.com
104169

## *DEDICATION*

Dedicated to the one who broke my heart for opening my eyes to my good in this world. Mikayla for pushing me to pick up a pen and get past that broken heart, you're amazing. Jason Johnson for editing, driving the crazy twists, and putting up with me for a year of madness. Finally family some born some blood (Lynn, Mom, Dad, Sister, Cooper, Alex, Waylon, Darla, Linda) for standing behind whatever it is crazy I decide I want to try. Without all of you I wouldn't have even dared a venture of this sort.

# PART 1

Landon's life had fallen together and then apart in a matter of days. His full ride to college now washed down the drain with responsibility. Why him? Why her? "It wasn't supposed to be forever," he screamed out at the fresh open sky. A sky that now made him feel so miniscule in the grand scheme of things. It was the same sky that just hours before he felt he could reach out and squeeze in his hands. A new revelation in the folds of life as life had just begun, and from hero to zero, his entire being was twisted in knots. For the first time since he could remember, he was scared to death. Tears streamed down his face. Mother, the whole town, and, hell to anyone that mattered, he felt like he let them all down.

Life was majestically simpler back when that angel swooped down from the rifts of heaven and placed herself among his side. Heather used to crane her pretty little head to peek glances at her small town hero while she was cheering him from the sidelines and was always in trouble for watching the gridiron frenzy behind her. She was only a cheerleader because she wanted to be closer to him. She loved the essence of everything he was and she wanted to be a part of everything he was. Heather was an angel in her daddy's eyes and she could do no wrong. She was 5'7", 125 pounds of American angel. Her glossy, deep blue eyes complimented her perfect, pale skin and that red hair gave off a hint of a spark nobody saw; nobody, but him that is. She would ride this scholarship as well as her ticket out of that small aged town.

Heather walked beside him throughout the majority of their whole high school venture. Hand in hand, they experienced it all. From the college visits of UCLA to his national letter of intent; he caught passes, broke records, gave the old men something to talk about over coffee, and most of all he had a way out. A full ride to college because he was fast and dropped absolutely nothing. These were the two skills that had made him a god and a legend in his hometown. Three touchdowns in the State Championships, one of which came off the longest kick return of

Christian county history. It was that feeling of being invincible he planned on keeping. From one small town to a whole state, and with a little luck, the pros. Landon clutched onto the dreams of being a god forever and Heather walked gracefully by his side the whole way, never knowing that life could instantly knock them off the path they were taking. Soon enough the mirage would dispel and the smoke would clear and life would hit them in the stomach hard enough you could hear the air dispatch from the lungs they filled.

Life was no longer about the grime of the game or the passion of the love . . . it was bigger than that . . . bigger than them. So he made that Pinto scream in mercy as the gravel and dust flew in untraceable directions out from underneath the rusty wheels. Earlier it had been a perfect day, a nice mountain morning fishing trip with the guys. It was one of the last real days before they dispelled into the world in separate directions. As each cold brew was replaced by a hole in the ice, they felt more like the world was theirs for the taking. That phone call knocked Landon back into sobriety, however, and now he was alone. Alone and making that rust bucket scream down to the corner store in town. He knew what he needed to buy. He knew what would solve all this and in just hours everything would go back to normal. He was running away from it all at a dead sprint. The first one had to lie . . . there could be no truth in what was running through his head now. All of it based off of what? What three dollars worth of plastic had told that angel before? That road seemed longer than ever before and everything seemed wide open now. From a god to an alien shot to a distant planet, he wasn't at home with anything now.

Tom's came into view and Landon pulled the ride into a screeching halt in front with the car coming to a rest parked crooked in the handicapped parking spot. "Hell, they can tow it," he thought to himself. It's the only thing that attaches me to that worthless father of mine anyway. The car was a gift from his father when he turned 16. It was a $300 junker his dad pulled out of his own junkyard. The place where his father stayed through birthdays, too inebriated to make it to his son's party. Only game he ever made it to was State and, even through the victory, all he was able to mutter is, "You shouldn't have dropped that third pass." Records broken and still he wasn't good enough for his dead beat alcoholic father. Aisle three was where the answer was in a little pink and white box with fifty cents worth of plastic inside. He knew because it was something that they had stumbled onto before. Just a joke, you know? Something that could never happen to a hero with his red-headed Cinderella. He picked up the product and began to briskly move to the counter knowing the answer would be his as soon as he got to Heather's house. Life would go back to normal and they would laugh during the first real college party of the year at how terrified he was. Landon paid for the product and talked to old Tom. It was polite, you know? Of course, Tom would want to ask him how it felt to be the first All-State player in 40 years from Christian county.

As Landon turned towards the door, it violently flung open and a man clad with a ski mask threw himself inside. You could feel the terror in his voice as he screamed, "Give me the money, you old geezer . . . I have a new mouth to feed and this fast food cook mess is not feeding the others as it is . . . . You, meat head, stay where you are," he said, waving the weapon in Landon's direction. "You're not the hero on this field." You could tell it was the man's first time as the villain and he was trembling as his finger toyed with the idea of pulling the trigger. He had to do it, didn't see any way out. He had new mouths to feed and a real man does anything to feed his kids. Landon took one step towards the disgruntled man and, out of nervousness, he pulled the trigger.

"You don't have to . . ."

The words were replaced by the crack of the explosion that propelled the round out the chamber and Landon tumbled aimlessly forward.

The crack of the gunshot had made everything, plain before, flash white. Landon desperately clutched his chest as the deep crimson poured out. The man had received all cash out of the small drawer and the small town god's world was closing in. He could hear distant sirens but they were simply too distant. Landon's last moments of life were accompanied with his whole life flashing before his eyes in a blur. First practice, first touchdown, first kiss. Was it really all tearing away like this? He would never learn the truth of the joy nine months later as the last thing he felt was a foot across the hand clutching what he had purchased minutes before. The bag slid across the floor in the skirmish as the man ran out the door into the hailing fire from police. It then bounced off the wall and out slid a receipt and a pregnancy test. A revelation and the answer to a world that no longer existed. A legacy of a god now fallen, resting on his unborn child. The carrier of his shattered dreams was now a bastard in this world that he no longer had control over. His last breath exhaled. It was all over and he never got to achieve more than his own father . . . never more than his father.

Jason Thomas never made it out of the parking lot. He was gunned down by officers of the law releasing the grocery bag full of musty cash as he, too, tumbled aimlessly to the ground. The cash spilled out of the bag and floated in the wind as people began gathering around to see what the commotion was about. The generic small town with small town ways took one on the chin that day and between the howling of the sirens and the birds singing a now mournful chirp, there was a sense of eerie silence.

Two deceased with more in common than anyone knew. Both perished from this world in a violent manner leaving behind a legacy for the unborn children; those bastard children who were to bear titles of their daddies without even knowing the touch of their sperm donors.

# PART 2

Heather hurled the phone across her small bedroom, where it violently shattered, and lay vibrating on the floor. She had just rang his cell phone and needed to hear his voice, but instead she got his stupid voicemail. She hadn't heard from him in three days. "Damn this cruel joke," she whispered aloud with a frantic chuckle. If they knew I was carrying his child, they wouldn't play childish games. Landon was a god; he didn't have the ability to break immortality now; no not now, now that she needed him . . . not that they needed him more than ever.

"Whatever," she shot at herself in the mirror as she threw on a track suit. "Come on biscuit," she called to her beagle that had been a birthday gift from Landon. "We're going to go find daddy. This joke has to be over by now." She had known for 48hrs now what had happened, but she was sure it was a cruel joke from his buddies as they were the type to do that sort of thing all the time.

"Man, that Jeremy Lawson should be an actor," she almost scolded the mutt as they walked briskly by the moonlight down the quiet street. He made it seem so real when he showed up that night and told a story of how Landon freaked out, eventually leaving their camping trip.

"He was in a real frenzy," Jeremy told her. "I'm sorry, Heather," he almost whispered. "He's gone." She couldn't remember how the conversation went exactly. She simply knew that she would get him after this was over.

Everybody in the small town of Quaintsville was shocked. How in their town could something tragic like this happen? It was a place where doors were left open at night so a breeze could pass through the unlocked screen door. Everyone was family and, fresh off state championships, the small town beamed with school pride. Nothing like this should happen and it was almost a daily shock to each citizen as they made that journey down the short Main Street and past Tom's and saw the yellow tape over the door. Tom's was now in sight for Heather and biscuit as well. Could they take down that stupid picture of him, she thought as she passed the vigil in front of Tom's? "If they are going to go along with this joke at least they could have picked a better picture," she stated in Biscuit's direction. She wished she had had his letterman jacket, but he took it on that fishing trip with him. He told her that her wearing it made it smell like her so it would remind him of her up at the cabin. If I had him or that jacket tonight, she had thought, I wouldn't be so chilly, never knowing she would never see the now crimson red stained jacket again; never smell the smell or feel the wooly feel of him again.

She was suddenly awakened and rushed herself to the bathroom. She wondered while she was puking if this was the baby or broken heart syndrome. What the hell am I thinking, she thought? "Broken heart syndrome? Really, Heather?" she mocked herself in the mirror. Three weeks had passed and it was beginning to dreadfully sink in, like concrete in the pit of her stomach. Landon was really gone; college was gone, everything gone except for what she carried inside. Still, nobody knew of the pregnancy. The pregnancy test had been kicked to the corner in the scuffle that happened at Tom's that day and she felt it would tarnish Landon's heroic image to that small town. Somehow, she felt as if when they found out they would be angry at him for leaving her and this unborn child behind. Heather knew she certainly was and she was mad he wasn't there to hold her hair back as she got to re-experience that morning's breakfast. She was scared. More scared than the day she found out and she felt as if she had been kicked in the teeth and her smile was broken. She walked back into her room, grabbed one of his state championship shirts, and pulled it on over her now growing breasts and expanding stomach. It still gave of his fragrance and she thrust herself into the bed as thoughts of him came pouring over her and she fell back to sleep in pools of sobs.

Another week had passed and Heather estimated she was two months into this mess. "Yeah, that's about how long ago it was," she thought and she remembered that drunken party like it was yesterday. She experienced these thoughts daily and it seemed every memory of him terrorized every second of every day. Today would be the day, she thought and I'll tell them know before church and that will give me a chance to break away from it. It was the Lord's Day and they honestly couldn't yell at her in church, she thought. She was only eighteen and carrying a deceased man's baby. Heather knew she was to be a failure to her parents and she hated to let them down. Another trip to the bathroom showed the morning's muffins. Those trips were mainstay now as she had problems keeping anything down. She slowly brushed her teeth, straightened her glowing hair as she began to think of a game plan of something to say. She ventured out into the living room. "Mom . . . Dad," her voice quivered as she spoke. "Can I speak with you?"

Her parents were shocked. Her father stood up, ripped a chilly six pack from the fridge, and disappeared in a flash, out of the house without a word. Seconds later she could hear his old Ford fire up and lurch violently out of the drive as he pressed it down the road. No church today she thought and she felt the weight of the world crushing down on her. She fell into her mother's arms in sobs.

"Honey, how long have you known this?" her mother whispered.

"I found out the day I lost him," she replied in a tone that was broken and barely audible.

Her mother brushed Heather's tear soaked hair out of her face and said, "Look at me, Heather Mae. Your dad's just surprised. He will be back. Don't worry about it. I know you're scared, baby, but we will just have to roll with the punches."

Heather was relieved they knew, but was crushed to see her father react that way. She didn't blame him, she thought, "I guess I'm no longer his little angel"

"Go get ready for church," Her mom stated. "I will make you an appointment first thing in the morning."

"Mom," she whispered through the sobs. "I'm scared"

"Me, too, angel," was her mother's only offer at comfort.

* * *

Three months passed and she was five months in. None of her clothes fit anymore. She didn't feel like dressing sexy, anyways. She awoke to an alarm now days instead of the mainstay reappearance of breakfast. She looked at herself in the mirror as she rubbed canola oil on her bulging stomach.

"Can't give mommy stretch marks," she whispered, talking to the fetus inside that bulge. It was her third monthly appointment, something that was beginning to be normal for her. All her friends were now off to college and she was still rolling out of her parent's bed. She was already growing used to the change in her life. Her daddy had somehow grown used to it as well and he peered in her door and looked down at his watch.

"Come on, honey. Today's the day we find out whether it's a football player or a cheerleader," he exclaimed, and she was surprised by the excitement in her father's voice. It felt good that he supported her after that six pack incident three months prior.

The hour long journey that now seemed to take days to the hospital went without incident. Her mother smiled at her as they stepped out of the car. Her parents were beaming with excitement.

"She looks like you, Lisa," her dad exclaimed when Heather placed her hand on the small of her back. "Your mother used to always stand like that when she was pregnant with you," he added.

"What do you expect, dad?" she snapped back. "I am a house wide now."

"You even sound like her," her father returned with the same intensity. The only reply she afforded him was a quick swat in the gut as he chuckled and opened the door inside. They were late getting to the hospital on this day. It was early December and the snow had slowed their journey from the country into that city hospital. She was called back almost instantly and began to go through the motions. Change into the puke green gown, hop up on the bed, and let the doctor do his job.

Dr. Anderson pushed his self into the room and greeted Heather with a smile. "You ready, young 'un?" he exclaimed. Minutes later, he glanced up from all the monitors and playfully shot up at her, "Five bucks and I'll tell you what's inside you."

"Shut up, you old fart," she answered with a smile.

"Young lady," the doctor looked up at Heather and her mother, "looks like Christian county is going to have another football player! With any luck, he will be just as good as his daddy."

What kind of luck is that, Heather pondered as she stared aimlessly up at the tiled ceiling? She wept quietly in her mother's soft embrace. "When will I wake up from this nightmare," was all she could think.

# PART 3

Heathers pregnancy created a new stir in that quaint little town. The old men discussed the possibility that he may be like his daddy. Hell, even earlier in the day Frank Hearst looked at her and exclaimed, "Best take care of that star you're carrying around. I hope he's like his daddy."

She just smiled and continued on with what she was doing. They didn't know of the pain she was going through. She lost everything in that handful of dreadful months. She woke up every day and stared down at the constant reminder of what she had lost months before. It had been eight months and she was huge. It had been eight months and the pain was still there. She still wore his class ring that he always promised to replace with diamonds. "I'll be your superhero, baby. We will be rich and have it all," he would always tell her. She missed his voice, his touch, his kiss, but all she had now to hold onto was what was inside.

Tom's had opened up but remnants of the vigil were still there. A lot of things had gone back to normal but the sting was still there. It was almost unbearable for Heather to be out in public. People always glared at her as if she were a monster. Everyone knew, as everyone always does in a small town, and everyone was excited. Everyone except for her and she felt bad for what she was carrying inside, really. How could he be expected to live up to his daddy's legacy when he hadn't even taken his first breath of oxygen yet?

"Damn this small town," she thought and she dreamed of a way out. She daydreamed a lot about how things used to be and how things were supposed to be. She should be in UCLA right now listening to him complain about all the work he had to do to get ready for pre-season. It was all in her head and she knew it. The reality was there; she was stuck in this small town carrying a kid and it was a damn bastard child at that.

* * *

She was awoken early with deep pains in her lower stomach. She was drenched in sweat and she called out to her mother. In a frantic rush, Lisa ran in the room.

"Honey, let's get you on your feet. We have to get to the hospital," her mother said in that calm tone mothers have. Inside, her mother was terrified. They still had four weeks left before the baby was due. All she could do was say a little prayer as she rushed around the house grabbing whatever she felt was needed. She finally got Heather to stumble to the Pontiac as she closed the door behind her, rushed to the other side of the car, and hopped in the driver's seat. She grabbed the gear selector and tried to force it in reverse.

"Mom! What in the hell are you doing?" Heather snapped.

"It won't go into gear," Lisa snapped back.

"Get the keys first, mother," Heather yelled. Lisa was embarrassed; she had forgotten to even grab the keys off the end table.

They tore out of the drive and out onto the interstate. Lisa was now flying down the same interstate Landon had flown down eight months ago. Heather was in the passenger seat clutching her lower stomach and moaning and crying. Neither of them said much as they were both terrified. The normal hour long drive took forty five minutes this time and Lisa whipped that Pontiac into the emergency vehicles only lane at the ER. Smoke rolled out from under the paint chipped hood as she flung the door open. She grabbed the first wheelchair she saw and whisked Heather into it. At this point, a commotion had already stirred and emergency room nurses took over.

"She's pregnant," Lisa called as they wheeled Heather away, "and four weeks early." Heather was whisked away before Lisa even shut the doors on the car.

All Heather could do was scream and stare at the ceiling. None of the faces around her were familiar and her body felt like it was imploding.

"Where is everyone at? Why the fuck am I always alone in this? Get my fucking mom!" She was exploding. She was furious and furiously terrified of what was happening. "Where's Doctor Anderson?" she questioned another.

"He's been called, honey, and both your parents are in the waiting room filling out paperwork," an older Nurse replied in a soft meaning to be soothing tone. The soothing tone had failed on Heather, though, and soon enough she just laid there in agony crying and clutching onto the necklace that had his class ring on it. She whispered his name and the world went white as she passed out from the fury of everything. The nurses continued working furiously around her.

Dr. Anderson rushed into the waiting room and straight to Lisa and Dan.

"She's in bad shape, Mr. and Mrs. Waterson," he said as he was flipping through his notes. "We're going to have to operate. Her body's going in shock and the guy inside says its go time."

"The guy inside," Lisa snapped. "That's my baby girl in there and you better do whatever you can to make sure my girl and my grandson are perfectly fine."

"Honey," Dan tried to sooth his wife but to no avail. This wasn't a soothing day, and she fell to her knees and prayed. It was the first time she had really prayed in awhile, but she squeezed her eyes shut as the tears began to fall. She prayed for her daughter and the team of doctors that were in charge of that girl.

"For eighteen years I have taken care of her and been in control and now I can't do a damn thing to help my baby," she whispered up to Dan. When she raised her eyes up to meet his she noticed a tear trailing down his face. It was the first time she had seen him cry and she realized he was just as helpless and torn as she was.

It seemed like hours had passed before the doctor returned. When he returned to Lisa he looked a million years more aged. Blood covered the scrubs he had been wearing and dotted the mask as he pulled it down.

"Lisa . . . . Dan . . . They both made it out of the cesarean alive," the doctor greeted them.

"Thank you, Jesus," Lisa whispered and couldn't help but throw her arms around the doctor. He pushed her briskly away and stared at the set of parents for what seemed an eternity.

"The next 24 hours are the most crucial. He's underweight and she's lost a lot of blood. Poor girl was all baby. She was just opening her eyes as we took him out of the room," he stated and turned and rushed away.

Dan embraced his wife with a hug and a kiss on the forehead and looked down at her. "Honey, God took care of her for us. It will be ok." He glanced up just in time to catch Landon's father stumbling into the waiting area. "What the . . ." Dan stated shocked and Lisa was now tracking the commotion. Lisa jolted in Frank's direction.

"What the fuck are you doing here?" she snapped at him.

"I'm here to welcome my grandson and my son's last mistake into this world," he shot back in her direction as he stumbled into a chair. "Not very Christian or ladylike of you is it, Lisa, to spout off 'FUCK' in this waiting room full of people? Stupid bitch," Frank responded, inebriated. Lisa was appalled to see him. She began to retaliate but Dan had cut her off by this point and tore her away and out into the cool air. They stood on the waiting room patio and just stared at each other.

Heather felt as if she had been hit by a steamroller as she managed to force her eyes open. Her son had just disappeared out of the operating room. He was hooked to all sorts of machines that rolled out a techno-like tone and she was still terrified. "Still alone," she thought to herself. She rubbed her deep blue eyes and winced as she felt the tension of the fresh staples in her stomach. "So much for the canola oil," she thought to herself, "Instead of stretch marks I get scars." "My luck," she thought, "I've got a scarred heart, a scarred mind, and now a scarred body." She drifted in and out of consciousness and did her best to come to terms with what had just happened.

"Where's my, Braylen?" she exclaimed. The nurses looked at her surprised Heather was even awake.

"Your parents are getting ready to meet you in your room now, honey," one of the nurses responded.

"No, you idiot," Heather said, "My son, Braylen. Is he alright? Where did you take him? Where can I find him?"

"They are cleaning him up, honey and he will be brought to your room when it's safe," the nurse reassured her. He then turned and called into the nurses' station, "Baby Waterson has a first name now."

"Waterson," Heather shot to the nurse, "His name is Braylen Maston. You know, Braylen? Like B-R-A-Y-L-E-N and Maston like his daddy Landon's last name."

The nurse, shocked, just laid the bed back and pushed her out into the hallway and in the direction of her room. As she was wheeled into her room, she opened her eyes just in time to catch two things: Landon's father was off to the right side of the door and the name of her roommate was Kareen Thomas. These sent her into confusion. It was only the second time in her life she had seen Landon's father and her mind frantically switched to Kareen Thomas. Thomas? That named seemed strangely familiar she thought as she drifted into unconsciousness.

# PART 4

Heather awoke and wondered if it had all been a dream. Her hand shot to her stomach and the staples were still there. She then slowly opened her eyes to see her mother and father sitting at her bedside. Her father stood up and walked over to her grabbing her hand. She just stared up at him astonished at what had taken place. It had all happened so suddenly in an intoxicating blur and she was trying to piece it all together. First, though, she wondered, "Am I really a mother?" and the thoughts were almost instantaneously answered as a nurse bound into the room.

"Well, hello, mommy," the nurse greeted Heather.

"Where's Braylen?" Heather asked in return.

"He will be in shortly. He truly is a beautiful baby," the nurse answered. She finished taking Heather's vitals and turned towards the door.

"Tell them, 'I'm sorry,' for the way I acted," Heather called to her.

The nurse halted at the door, turned around, and gave her a wide smile, "Honey, it's understandable after what you were going through. They deal with it every day."

"Deal with what?" Heather wondered as she was still unclear at what had really happened. She was in such a fog, she thought, and she once again resorted to reaching for Landon's class ring as she pondered like she had done countless times before.

"Where is it?" she asked her mother.

"Where is what, honey?" her mother followed up the question with another question.

"Landon's class ring! I have never taken that off! It's not here!"

"I haven't seen it, honey," her mother replied, wishing she had some clue as she knew the fury it would bring.

"Dammit," Heather whispered. Where was all this rage coming from, she wondered. Pregnancy must have changed me, she thought to herself. Heather was the quiet, all American girl and now she was cursing like a sailor. She wondered if her parents had heard her in that rage that she was in and wondered if she really said all those things because it all felt and looked like a dream. She was embarrassed at the way she acted and, once again, she began to cry, but this time she hurriedly wiped the tear away and scolded herself for letting it all get to her. She figured by now she would have been used to getting kicked while she was down.

A figure walked briskly through the door and Heather started to question once again about the ring but realized this was not a nurse at all. It was Landon's mother, Elizabeth. Lisa stood up and greeted her, but she continued walking straight for Heather. Her arms outstretched, she embraced Heather and started frantically apologizing.

"I'm sorry I didn't make it here sooner, daughter," she whispered in Heather's ear.

"It's ok. You're here now," Heather smiled at her in assurance. The two had grown incredibly close since Landon's death and Elizabeth was almost like Heather's mother. Who could have blamed them? After Landon's death all they had to hold onto was each other.

"Where's my grandson?" Elizabeth asked.

"I would like to know the same thing, Lizzy," Heather responded.

"Little sucker is in that room hooked up to all sorts of wires and ruckus," Frank mumbled as he stumbled into the room. "Looks like he's coming into this world where his daddy left off . . . . failing." This time he was much louder.

Heather was astonished and she began to speak, but was cut off by her father. Dan was a quiet man and always tried to avoid conflict, but this was enough, he thought. He jumped from the chair he was sitting in, pushed through the women, and in one motion he swung and hit Frank with a hard right cross. Blood began to ooze out of Frank's nose as he tumbled to the floor. At that time, nurses rushed in to see the commotion. Dan didn't even notice the attention, and he kicked Frank hard in the stomach and knelt down beside him.

"If I ever catch you bad mouthing my daughter or my grandson again, I will kill you. Day or night I don't care who's around. That is my baby girl and my grandson. Frankly, it's all you have left of your son and, dammit, you pushed him around enough, too. That boy was a hero to this . . . ." He was cut off.

Security had pulled Dan back to his feet and began ushering him out of the room and into the hallway. Dan did not put up a fight, but merely turned and reintegrated what he had said before.

"Frank, I promise to almighty God I will kill you". Frank, astonished, was lifted to his feet and taken to the Emergency Wing.

"This one's going in for public intoxication after we patch up that nose," the security guard told the three women. "Anyone want to claim him?" Lisa, Elizabeth, and Heather all simply stared at him, astonished. The guard nodded, grinned, and then turned and walked out of the room. "Bunch of backwoods folks," he chuckled to himself under his breath. The three women didn't hear him, however, and continued staring at each other in silence for what seemed to be an eternity.

The silence was broken by a nurse that walked in pushing an incubator. "Braylen?" Heather questioned.

"Yes, honey. Here is your son," the nurse replied. Heather's face instantaneously lit up with her old smile. He was the most beautiful thing Heather had ever laid eyes on. She was excited to see that he had her hair. But that nose, that was definitely his father's nose, Heather thought. He was perfect to her, but oh so tiny and still hooked up to machines.

"How is he doing?" Elizabeth and Lisa simultaneously questioned the nurse.

"He's a lot better than to be expected this early," the nurse responded. "He really wants to be out of this incubator. We were able to get him off oxygen early this morning."

"Can I hold him?" Heather questioned.

"Not yet, honey. But I bet by tomorrow morning he will be here to greet you eyes wide. It's unbelievable how fast he's fighting through this," the nurse responded.

"His daddy was a fighter, too," Elizabeth stated with a smile and for the first time in awhile Heather shared that smile. It was almost as if the baby had replaced what she lost when she lost Landon. It was like somehow Landon was still alive.

Heather realized that it was the first time she heard anyone speak of Landon and it didn't drive her to tears. It was a strange feeling to see this baby with a head full of hair that matched hers. It was a feeling she had never experienced before. Her mom had warned her that it would be like this the first time she saw her own child, but it was far more than her mother experienced, she thought. This was her only connection to Landon. She just sat there and stared down at him with a shy smile and the rest of the world disappeared. In the midst of all the fury of everything around her, she was happy and she wanted so badly to hold him and just kiss him all over to let him know that mommy was there and would never let anything bad happen to him. She knew in her head at that moment that everything she had been through had been worth it for him. All the tears, all the mornings spent in the bathroom, all the glares from folks around town. It was worth it all now. She just wished Landon was there to experience it all. She shot a glance towards the ceiling and thought to herself, "What are you thinking, Heather? Landon's there and he's looking down on us both right now. You know they were right," she thought, "with any luck he will be just like his father." She just hadn't decided if that was her luck or Braylen's luck they were talking about.

The nurse then spoke up and interrupted Heather's gaze upon the child. "Honey we have to take him back now. I just wanted you to see him. He's a beautiful child, isn't he?"

"He sure is," was Heather's only response as the nurse wheeled him back out.

"So we're grandmas now, Elizabeth," Lisa said.

"Oh I know! At least were not ancient. I feel she's going to need some help with this one and, you know, he will get plenty of spoiling," Elizabeth responded.

"I'm sorry for Frank barging in here . . . ." She began to apologize, but Heather cut her off and her sweet contained smile flashed as she spoke in her childlike sweet twang.

"It's ok, Lizzy. Just promise me that Braylen's next grandpa that you find won't be a complete douche bag."

"Honey, I wish you wouldn't talk like that," Lisa chimed in.

"Lisa, she's fine. But, ladies, who knew Dan was capable of something like that," Elizabeth chuckled.

"Yeah," Heather added "who knew?"

The three sat and conversed for awhile about life and what the future held for Heather and the baby. The nursery wasn't even complete yet, but they would make do with what they had while Dan finished it. Eventually, Heather grew tired and felt she just wanted to be alone to sort everything out.

"Mom, Liza? Can I have some alone time now?" she asked. "It's been a crazy day and, mom, you need to go find my father and make sure our boxer isn't up on charges." All three of them had a quick laugh and the mothers hugged Heather and walked into the hall still discussing that day's commotion.

"Rough day, huh?" a deeply accented voice asked from around the curtain.

Heather had forgotten she even had a roommate and she blushed, glad she was separated by at least that curtain. Kareen Thomas then shyly stepped around the curtain.

"This is your first, huh? It's always exciting the first time. I have three of my own and now a baby girl Stephanie," Kareen stated. Heather was still surprised at the idea that this woman heard all the commotion.

"I'm sorry for all that," Heather apologized, but Kareen shook it off and walked up to Heather, her hand outstretched.

"Kareen Thomas."

"Heather Waterson" The two exchanged greetings. "Looks like we will be spending a couple days together," Heather said, trying to be polite.

"Yeah, I just wish Jason was here to see her. Here, I found this, and I heard you talking, I figured it may be yours," Kareen responded and handed Heather Landon's class ring. Heather clutched onto the ring with excitement. She had completely missed the name or relativity in the name that Kareen had just spouted.

# PART 5

The rest of the day was uneventful. It was the most relaxation she had been able to get in the last 72 hours and she was thankful for that. She needed the rest. She wondered what was so odd about the girl next to her. She had seen the nurses bring Kareen her child and such, but that was her only visitors. Heather didn't want to pry because she barely knew the woman. She just knew something was off. From the moment they exchanged glances it didn't seem right. Something about this woman had not set well with her. She seemed polite, about 24 years of age, she thought. Some wrinkles in her face, but hell, with three kids, Heather thought, that's to be expected. She just couldn't place what was giving her so much discomfort in this woman that seemed so upbeat. It still puzzled her as she drifted off to sleep only to be awoken by the checks of the nurses from time to time.

The next morning she was awoken bright and early as promised. Her parents and Elizabeth were there already and were happy to greet her.

"How ya feeling, honey?" her father asked.

"Oh, like I've been hit by a train, pops," she playfully replied.

"They brought Braylen in earlier, but you were sleeping. No one held him. We felt it was best if you were first," her mother added. Heather sort of felt crushed that she had missed him. Her father could read the expression on her face and stood up to see if they could bring him back. About a minute later, he returned with a nurse trailing.

"Here you go, honey," the nurse greeted Heather as she handed Braylen over. He seemed more gorgeous than before, and she beamed with pride. When she thought it couldn't get any better, he slowly opened his eyes, blinked once, yawned, and then looked up at her. His eyes were the same glossy blue as hers and she knew she was staring into her future.

It truly was amazing that after only 48 hours the little one had made it off of all the machines and tubes. He was four weeks early, but he wasn't entirely too small. Heather truly was all baby for the last month of her pregnancy and some had predicted she would go early anyways. She was glad, however, that he had arrived early. Throughout all the damn drama, she had just wanted the date to arrive faster. It seemed like the hands of father time had slowed down and it still was all a shock to her, however, how something like that had been formed. How a simple choice over too much alcohol could change her future with such a vast effect. She had lost so much of how she wanted everything to be. But somehow, she felt bad for her friends off at college. She knew that it would be years before they could experience anything like this. She knew that it wasn't a mistake now, that this is where she was meant to be.

"It's going to be hard little guy," she whispered down to Braylen, "but we're in this together and I'll never leave your side." She then kissed his tiny little forehead.

The rest of the day was spent with people coming and going. Heather's dad had left early to go work on the nursery, but she was ok with that. She knew it needed to be done. She really just wanted to be left alone with Braylen, but she knew that people would come to see her. She was excited to present him to every person as if he was some sort of trophy. Everyone agreed he was the most beautiful baby that they had seen. He seemed to be a replicate of Landon except for the red hair and eyes. She loved him. Oh, how she loved him. It pained her that Landon was not able to be there to see him. She spent most of the day between visits whispering things to the baby about his father. She had no intentions of ever loving another. She kept her promises. She could remember so clearly the night they had spent on the river bank where they had made a pact to love each other forever. It was the most romantic night that you could picture and thoughts of it made her smile. The stars were so clear that night as they stared up at the open sky and talked of forever. Everything was clear to her in full landscape view but now it was all gone. Even though he was gone, she would keep up her end of the deal and she would find a way to make sure Braylen knew exactly who his daddy was. She owed it to him. She felt she owed it to everyone.

Heather was drifting in and out of sleep when she heard him start to cry. She awoke because it sounded so distant. He was on the changing table and Kareen was changing him along with her girl.

"What are you doing?" Heather shot, surprised at how defensive she had become.

"I'm changing him, girl. These first few days are going to be gross. Hell, the next year will be gross." Kareen was explaining with a smile, but Heather cut her off.

"He is my baby. I will change him."

"I'm sorry. It's just you were sleeping so peacefully and he started to whimper when I was changing Steph. I'm sorry. I didn't mean to upset you".

It was a valid explanation, but Heather was still up in arms. Kareen could see the frustration spreading across Heather's face, so she began to explain further.

"I know how you're feeling, Heather. I've been there before He's your first and you don't want anyone to touch him except for you. He's your pride and joy and, hunny, he always will be, but give it a year and you will be begging others to want to hold him. Trust me"

Heather didn't have an answer. She just stood up, walked over to the table the two babies were on, and finished the job of changing her son. She kissed him and picked him up and he seemed to flash a small shy smile to her, almost as if to say, "Way to go, mom." Heather felt a rush of embarrassment because she knew she had overreacted.

"Sorr . . . ." she began to apologize. Kareen cut her off, gently touched her arm, and walked out of the room with her child, humming along the way. Heather could tell she was experienced and had been down this path before. She was once again thankful to be alone as she was left there with Braylen. She nursed him with a small bottle and rocked him to sleep. Soon she was there herself.

"Wake up, sleepyhead," the nurse said as she opened the curtain. Heather began clutching for Braylen. "He's in the nursery getting weighed and fed," the nurse, catching the reaction, explained.

"Oh," Heather responded and she was greeted by her mother.

"Hey, honey, how was the night?" her mother asked.

"Oh, good. It feels so good to hold him and feed him. First diaper change was interesting though," Heather began to explain. Her mom had no idea, however, as to why the first diaper change was so interesting. Heather didn't care to explain either.

"So do you want to go home today?" the nurse broke the awkward silence.

"Today?" Heather exclaimed. "Already?!" She couldn't believe it.

"Heather, you've been here for five days already," her mom offered an explanation. "Braylen is doing so well, it's a miracle really," her mother continued. Heather feeling that oh so now normal feeling of embarrassment cut her off.

"I knew that, mother!" Everyone knew she really didn't. It was at that time she realized that she was alone in the room with her mother. "Where's everyone at," Heather questioned.

"Well, your fathers at home putting the finishing coats on the nursery. Everything's moved in there now. He won't be able to stay there tonight, but we didn't figure you would like him to anyways. Liza is there helping him. Everyone in town is so excited for you to come home, honey," her mother answered.

"Well, let's go home then," Heather said with a wide smile.

* * *

The drive home seemed surreal and Heather kept looking over her left shoulder at the angel lying asleep in the back seat. He slept the whole way home and the two chatted as the miles home clicked across the odometer. Lisa was glad to see the excitement Heather held and that smile shining on Heather's face was somehow the brightest she had ever seen it. She then was able to come to the same realization that Heather had found earlier. Everything would be ok and she thanked god for this.

"What the . . . ." Heather's voice trailed off as she watched the sign go by. "Welcome home, Braylen," was attached to the county line sign.

"We've got a lot of help from the community, Heather," her mom explained. "You know Landon was a hero to everyone, honey, and that's his kid, too. Braylen is saving this old town from those bitter memories of that day eight months ago," Her mother continued.

Heather was astonished by all this. All the blue and yellow balloons and the signs people had lined Main Street with seemed like a mirage. It was almost like the time when they welcomed Landon's football team back from state. Heather didn't know that this was bigger than that. That day eight months ago that town lost a hero, lost its spark, lost the youthfulness of school spirit. It seemed that when Landon had been ripped away from that town, everything else disappeared as well. Braylen was the new Landon. He was the hope for the town and they needed him to replace that empty pit the murder had caused. The boy was about to be thrown into a legacy that was almost impossible for anyone to replace and he couldn't even talk yet.

# PART 6

The first five months had skirted by and Heather felt as if she could see him growing every day. Braylen had filled the void in her heart, but not in its entirety. Today would be just as hard as the day it happened and she knew as soon as she awoke the pain it would hold for her. It was the anniversary date of Landon's death, and it was time for her to relive that agony all over again. The last year of her life had blown by and with Braylen here he was able to take her mind off of most the madness. But not today. Today it weighed on her and she knew it would take all the strength she had to get through. It was the first time in a while she had been to his grave and the trip out to the grave was a long one. It was driven in complete silence except for the birds chirping and the rumble of the car as it pushed down the back road. Braylen would throw in some chuckles or blurts here and there, but Heather was left alone with her thoughts and it was like the pit inside her had opened up again. She was struggling to be strong. She knew she had to be for that baby sitting in the backseat.

Even though, she fought back tears as she pulled up to the gravesite. She wasn't surprised to see people had already arrived at the ceremony and was actually relieved. She never wished to be the first one there, anyways. She knew if she had to go it alone she wouldn't be able to fight back the tears. This was supposed to be a celebration of the short, but amazing life her hero had lived before that dreadful day, only a year prior, and she didn't want to ruin it with tears. She rubbed off the few that had managed to seep their way out of her tear ducts and checked her make up in the rearview mirror before she opened up the door. She then walked around the front of the car and to the passenger back seat. She reached down and picked up Braylen, forced a smile, and then took the long trek down those familiar pavers to meet the crowd that was already there. It was made up of about 30 people at this time, not all of which she knew, which was odd for a small town.

She knew he was a hero to them, but never realized how many people it had affected. She gave a quick smile as everyone was noticing her walking up. She then managed to find some of his old football buddies and mingled in so she at least felt like she wasn't an alien. She felt in her head, though, that she was the only one that belonged there. She was the only one that really knew him and really had to deal with the pain of his death every day. She regretted agreeing to do this and the pain she knew she was going to strangle herself through. It appeared to her that no one really wanted to focus on the reality of the death anymore and that Braylen was just going to push it away, like masks over a deep scar that she had to bear every day.

"We are here today for remembrance," the pastor began, "of a young man who changed this town, changed the way we thought, and how we looked at things. Landon was a bright young soul with a grasp on life and it was ripped away from him all too fast. This, however, is a celebration of remembrance and not mourning. For, we should not mourn for Landon because he is with father god now. Landon, like I said, was a hero to this small town. Everyone seemed to look up to him and he was in touch with God. Some of his accomplishments were the first to be had in this county in 40 years. He will be dearly missed by us all, but to really learn about Landon, we can only ask one person. A lady who probably knew him better than he knew himself. The same lady whom he fathered the child with," he paused, glanced at Braylen, and continued with a small muffled laugh, "that is giving me that ornery grin." The pastor then paused, chuckled, and took a breath. "Now I'd like to introduce his lady with whom he fathered a child. The child that brings hope to this small town so that one act of violence will not tear us down." He slowed his speech with the last sentence making sure to put emphasis on every word so that it sank in. "Heather, will you please come up here?" he asked and Heather began the long trek to the podium. This was the moment she dreaded and every eye weighed on her as she made her way to the podium feeling as if her knees were jello and wishing she could wake up.

"Hello, you all," She greeted with a forced smile. She felt paralyzed as they all eyed her. "So what do I say and how do I say it?" she questioned. "I guess I could tell you about Landon. As you all know, he was a hero to this town. He was a hero to you all, but he was far more than that as well." She paused for a brief moment, lost a battle with a tear, and continued as it ran down her check, a trace of mascara following closely behind. "Landon was a wonderful man. Full of life and full of love. I don't believe I will ever find anyone that could even compare in the smallest manner to Landon. We met when we were six at vacation bible school and even though I had 'cooties' he never left my side. We were together almost daily since then and we should be together now . . . ." Her voice trailed off as she began to sob. Her tone had changed now, "How am I to celebrate losing the one concrete thing I had in my life? What do you people really expect me to say up here, that I know he's in heaven and smiling down on me? Well, it's not about what you people feel and what he was to this town. You didn't know him! You knew the part he let you see and now it's all gone. All your fucking state championship bullshit and what you held onto him for. You used him and now he's not here when I need him for this baby that I wake up to every morning. A celebration . . . .?" She was in a rage now and losing control. Her face was tinted grey now as the mascara began to cover her cheeks. "Fuck this! I can't do this . . . ." She stared at the ground the whole way to her car. "I guess I ruined the celebration," she exclaimed to Braylen as she buckled him into the car seat. She then wiped her tears off his face, kissed him, and shut the car door.

"Are you ok?" a familiar voice questioned as Heather turned around.

"Kareen?" Heather exclaimed, shocked coming face to face with the woman she had shared a room with five months earlier. "What are you doing here? Do you want to celebrate as well? All these fucking people! Can't you just leave me and my baby boy alone? Seriously, what do all of you want? Landon's dead! Nothing we do will bring him back, so just leave me the . . . ."

She was cut off by the sudden embrace of Kareen and she lost control of the tears. She got lost in the sobs until she found herself wanting answers. "Wait, I've never seen you around here before. What are you doing here?" Heather questioned.

"I'm sorry for scaring you, hun. I live right down the road. I was walking to try to get rid of the flub that Steph gave me," Kareen explained. Heather wondered what effect it was this girl had on her, but she still couldn't place it. Instead of focusing on it she just brushed it aside.

"Well, do you care if we walk with you?" Heather questioned her. "I'll get his stroller out of the back. I could use the fresh air after all this."

"Sure. I could use a companion now that it's just me and her," Kareen explained as Heather pulled Braylen back out of the car. Her statement never sparked the curiosity it should have in Heather and the two turned for the road and started to walk. "So, tell me about you," Kareen questioned. "What are you doing out here and what was all that about? Who is Landon?"

"It's a long story," Heather tried to circumvent the question. "I hate that the only times you've seen me I've been a mess," Heather answered with a small chuckle.

"Well, it's only us, our babies, and the birds out here and, well, hunny you only seem half crazy, but you are pushing it," Kareen joked, "so I'm all ears".

"Landon was my world," Heather began. "I knew him forever and he was my first everything. First kiss, first love, first date. You know, first everything. He was basically my world. We, I mean he, had a full ride scholarship to UCLA to play football. We were going to use that to get out of this tiny town and have a life that you dream of. I had missed my period and took a pregnancy test. Well, you know the answer to that is sitting in this stroller in front of me. When I called him about it, freaked him out, but understandably because he had everything in front of him with the scholarship and all. I wish I would've just waited and told him in person, but I couldn't. He was away and I couldn't bear keeping it from him. Well, long story short, he didn't believe me and he freaked out. Drove to a gas station to get a new pregnancy test. He never made it out. It was a year ago today. He was shot as a man tried to rob the gas hole in town that Landon was buying the test at. He was everything to this small town and this was supposed to be a celebration for his life, but I sort of ruined it with my fit. I bet they will never look at me the same," Her voice trailed off. "None of them have ever seen me so much as frown before, let alone spaz like I did."

Kareen interrupted her and almost demandingly questioned, "He died exactly one year ago?"

"Yeah," Heather responded, sort of shocked. Kareen's only response was a nervous glance and then she stared intently at the ground. Braylen interrupted the awkward moment as he began to whine.

"Let's turn around so you can get him home before night," Kareen offered.

"Yeah," Heather responded, "I better get back before they start to worry about me."

\* \* \*

The whole drive home Heather tried in angst to figure out what had made that one detail make everything so awkward. Why would the fact that it happened exactly one year ago startle Kareen? She had to figure this out. She replayed every time she had talked to the Kareen, but she still struggled to place it. Everything about Kareen seemed completely normal except for the circumstances they had met and how the girl showed up. Heather felt she had to be the problem and was overreacting about everything. About the diaper change incident and the whole spaz incident she had had just hours before. Besides, Kareen was only a few years older than Heather and she was a pretty girl. She was polite on top of that. But even still, for some reason, Heather felt she shouldn't trust the girl as if she were a thief that had taken something from her. She didn't really know what the truth held, however, and she tried to push it out of her head. She turned up the radio a bit because Braylen liked it. "Oh well, Bub," she said as she glanced back to check on Braylen. "I hope we see more of her so I can place this feeling I have. I have to know what's got me trippy about her and show her that mommy's not as crazy as she seems lately."

The way the two women had crossed paths was truly unconventional, but Heather was clueless. She had no idea just what she had stepped into. She just continued pressing the miles taking her closer to home. She began to sing to Braylen every song that played on the radio. She watched the sun as she sang. Each minute it seemed to drop a little more and she couldn't be more thankful. She was glad that day was over although she knew she would have to give some type of explanation to everyone for the fit she had had earlier. She looked up in her rearview and a small smile crept across her face as she saw that boy sleeping like a rock in the back seat. "Hell with 'em," she whispered. "Clueless bunch, anyways."

# PART 7

The miles home seemed to stretch forever, but Heather didn't mind. The one thing she loved about the small town was the sunset, and tonight's was a gorgeous one, she thought to herself. At least the end of her day would end in something beautiful, because that day had been a wreck. She knew that she would have to relive this pain on this day every year. She wasn't looking forward to it, but she knew with Braylen, at this point, she could make it through anything. Soon enough, that familiar old town crept into view and she began to slow the car down to a crawl through the town. Everything was the same as it always was in that town and she prayed that once Braylen got a little older she could go to college. Hell, online at least. She had to escape from that place. At this point, all it held for her were haunting memories.

The driveway came into view and she swung the vehicle in. She grabbed Braylen out of the backseat and walked in the door.

"How was it, Honey?" her mother asked as she stepped inside.

"It was a disaster, momma," Heather began. "Let me take him in here to lie down and we will talk about it."

"Ok, Hun. Let me help. I missed him today" The two walked through the house to the blue and green nursery. Pictures of Landon hung on the wall so that the little guy could see his daddy. It was Heather's idea of course, as she wanted to keep Landon as Braylen's father. There was even a miniature jersey hung on the wall with Landon's number. One of the many visitors from town brought it as a gift and even though she hated seeing it, she hung it anyways as a polite gesture. She sat back in the old rocking chair as her mother laid Braylen on the changing station and began to change him. She stared at all her surroundings and wondered if she would really raise him alone. It had only been a year and the pain was still very much a bottomless pit in her stomach, but she knew Braylen needed some sort of father figure in his life.

"Let's talk about it," her mother broke Heather's train of thought as she laid Braylen into the bed.

"It was just a disaster mother. They expected it to be a celebration of his life, and you know it tortured me to go out there, to see the damn picture of him catching that winning pass. This town used him! They idolized him and really.... Well, I was standing up at the podium and I was putting on the normal rehearsed 'I'm happy I knew him' speech, but I just snapped."

"What do you mean, 'snapped'?" her mother questioned.

"Well, like I said, I was doing good, but I just sort of went off. I told them all that. I told them that I thought they used him. And, mom, I'm sure you will hear about it, the language got more colorful the deeper the rage I fell into. I just don't know where it's all coming from, mom. The first curse word I ever said, and I swear to this, was in the Delivery room of that hospital. This has just all changed me and I hate it, but I know I will make it through." Her mother began to speak, but Heather cut her off, "You know the woman that I was roomed with at the hospital? I ran into her after my rage." Her mother shot her a look of concern. "She asked about why we were all gathered at the cemetery, and I told her the story. She seemed really concerned with the fact that it was exactly one year ago. Things got really awkward after that and I came home," she finished.

"I've never been comfortable with that girl," her mother started. "Have you ever thought it was weird that she had his class ring. Where did she find it at? Also, her kid didn't have a father, either. I normally don't judge people, but something about her just caught me the wrong way"

"I know me, too," Heather interrupted her in almost a shout. "She's a nice girl and all, but something about her is just off and I don't get it."

"Me either, Hunny. Me, either," her mother responded and walked out of the room. Heather, left there with her own thoughts, began to rake everything over in her head again as she watched Braylen sleep. She knew life had to change from where it was at. She was 19, a widow in her mind, and no education. She was nowhere near where she wanted to be and she knew that she needed to change it, not for her, but them. She and Braylen needed a change. Maybe just maybe, she was recounting her previous thoughts; she would find someone new to try to use as a father for Braylen so that things could get better for the both of them. Yeah, that's it, she thought, I'll find him a daddy.

* * *

The next morning she awoke and decided to try to sell to her mother the ideas that had been on her mind the night before. "Mother, I think I'm going to try to go out on a date," she started to explain.

"What?" her mother said as she choked on her toast. "Why would you want to do that, you have Braylen to worry about and it's only been a year...."

Heather cut her mother off, "I don't want to replace Landon, mother. Hell, we know nobody could ever replace him. You don't know what it feels like, though, to drive around all alone." Tears slowly started streaming down her face. "Mom, Braylen will need a father figure in his life and I need someone to hold onto. You don't know what it's like to lose the love of your life. You don't know the pain every time I see Braylen smile, I see Landon smile." Her voice raised now, "Just understand, mother, that I only want what's best for my child. I know you have to understand that and, dammit, this isn't getting it. It's been a year and nothing is getting easier. NOTHING!"

Her mother was shocked at what she just heard. That wasn't her baby girl talking anymore and she got to witness the new evil side everyone in town was talking about. She couldn't find any way to blame her daughter though and she knew what Heather was saying made sense.

"Honey, I understand," crept hesitantly out of Lisa's mouth. Both were equally surprised to hear it. Heather welcomed it and skipped back to the nursery to wake Braylen up to start the day.

"Whew, I'm glad that one's over," she expressed to no one in particular as her phone rang.

"Hello?" Heather answered.

"Is this Heather?" a familiar voice questioned.

"Why, yes. Who is this?" Heather returned the question already knowing the answer.

"This is Kareen. I was wondering if you would like to go get some coffee and take a stroll around town. I need to get out of this house."

"Why, sure," Heather responded.

"I'll pick you up in about half an hour. Sound good?" Kareen stated and instantaneously hung up not giving Heather a chance to respond. How does she know my number Heather wondered, and better yet, how does she know where I live? She ran around the house to get everything ready. It was a very normal routine now really: grab Braylen's diaper bag, pack a few extra outfits just in case, and, last step, prep herself in the mirror. The last step was a new one. Maybe I'll see someone while we are walking around, she thought to herself. Better not rush it, her brain countered the thought. She knew that no one would be able to replace Landon. A horn honk blared in the drive way and Heather waltzed out the door with Braylen in tow.

The drive to the coffee shop in town was a short one. As the drive began the two only exchanged silence. The babies, however, seemed to strike up a conversation of their own which seemed to be contagious.

"They seem to get along well," Heather broke the silence.

"Yes, I was figuring that we should start hanging out more," Kareen answered. "We're both about the same age and in the same situation really."

"Same situation? What do you mean?" Heather questioned.

"Heather, we need to talk," Kareen quickly responded. The rest of the drive to the coffee shop was spent in an eerie silence.

# PART 8

The car finally crept to a halt outside the familiar coffee shop. Both females got out, and Kareen shot a forced smile in Heather's direction. Both of them knew that whatever happened next would most likely be a defining point in the relationship. The girls walked inside and grabbed a cup of coffee.

"I love this place," Heather once again tried to make conversation.

"Yeah, it's the first place me and Jason passed when we were passing through this area," Kareen answered.

"So you haven't been here long then, have you? I know I haven't seen you in the area until the day of the funeral. How did you know where I lived, how did you know my number, and how did you get Landon's ring? Ah, look at me freaking out on you all over again. First, I . . . . I want to apologize for the way you have seen me all these times. I really am a good person and polite. Just so you know, my life has been a wreck since Landon's death. I'm so lonely now a days and I feel it's too fast to move on, but at the same time I really don't want to sleep alone for the rest of my life. Look at me again, getting so off track. I'm sorry," Heather said in her sweet country twang. "You had something you wanted to talk about before I got us off subject."

"Well, let's get our coffee first before we get too deep into anything, Heather. I was thinking the other day and I have a story to tell you as well. We have more in common and are connected in a way that I don't think you could ever dream."

"Ok," Heather responded in a shocked tone. Kareen had put her down again, she thought as she ordered her coffee and a small glass of milk for Braylen.

The two stepped outside in the fresh air and began to walk down the old cobblestone side walk. "I have a story to tell you, Heather, about a man named Jason Thomas," Kareen began in a questioning voice. She took a deep breath and then continued as they walked. "I met Jason Thomas when I was six years old just like you had met your Landon. We were both kids in New York at the time. We were both middle class and a gated suburban area was where we called home. Jason was always there for me, but we drifted away when we were about 17. He chased after the high school prom queen, and even though I don't look it now, I was quite nerdy at that time. He had told me it would never be more than friends, but I had other ideas. You know how a girl holds on to hope?"

"Yeah," Heather answered in a whisper.

"Well, turns out that when Jason was at a party with the Prom Queen slut, they got drunk, as high school kids do, and she was pregnant. You could imagine how it crushed me when I found out. Sure enough, nine months later, popped out twins. I lost all hope for the love of my life."

The conversation was interrupted as they crossed. A kid in older model pickup truck about hit them as he ran the stop sign.

"Fucking, punk," they screamed towards the speeding vehicle in unison. They turned to each other with raised eyebrows.

"I guess we do have something's in common, huh," Heather said with a nervous chuckle. The two turned, continuing their journey as the babies once again became talkative.

"They do, too," Kareen responded.

"Your story," Heather stated.

"Yes, where was I?" Kareen's voice trailed off as she grew deeper in thought, "Oh, yes. Jason and I," she exclaimed. "Well, as I was saying, Jason got the prom queen slut pregnant with twins and I thought all my chances were down the drain. But I had hope. Things weren't working out for them and I had one thing on my side. He trusted me like he trusted no one else, so I took special time to give him the special attention. As soon as things got rough, she split for some drug dealer and left him with the kids. He was crushed, but Jason was a good guy and he began to raise them on his own without a mother figure. He worked two jobs while I stepped in and babysat the kids for him. I was only 19 myself, and I didn't have the money to go off to college. I was just a small town waitress going nowhere in life. The days grew longer and eventually I moved in with Jason. It was exactly what I wanted and the whole 'just friends' thing soon developed into what I had dreamed of all of high school. I was his princess and he was my prince charming. Sound familiar?"

Heather nodded and gave a quick, "Oh yeah, I know exactly where your coming from."

"Well, like you, I was going to use Jason to get out of that small town. We were going to make something of ourselves. So I talked him into trying to get a job down here in Tennessee. I had always heard about the Nashville area. It just seemed like a perfect little country place to get away from everything. Well, we packed up everything but on the day we were getting ready to go, I found something out. Instead of starting life in Tennessee with two children, it would be three. I was so excited to get out of that area that I didn't tell Jason. I knew that if he knew it would ruin our trip and I would be stuck in god awful New York, raising my kid in the melting pot of public school. I wanted so much more for my kid than to see the gang violence at school every day. So I didn't tell him that day. I figured I could just wait until we got to Tennessee and, yeah, I knew he would be mad, but I could deal with it. It would be worth getting out of that dreaded city with all the pollutants. I couldn't stand that place."

"Oh, I understand what you're saying there," Heather interrupted her. "I can't wait to get out of this place."

"I swear to you, hun, anywhere you go, you're going to want to end up right back here. There is no better place for you and your baby than right here. Believe me, I know better. I've seen it and I've been there. You haven't."

"Your story," Heather quickly interrupted the lecture before it could digress any further.

"Yes, my story," Kareen gave into Heather's desperate fleeing from the conversation. "Well, like I said the last two times," she paused with a chuckle, "me and Jason jumped on that interstate and the miles began to fly. It really was a smooth trip and I will remember almost every mile of it. His light tan and deep brown eyes, I could soak up his scent. It was just me, him, and the toddlers in the back seat. Life was really about to begin for me, but I had a secret. You know I was pregnant and it was beginning to eat at me that I had such a life changing secret and I held it inside. We woke up one morning at a little Holiday Inn about twenty minutes outside of this town. As I was pulling the kids out of bed and getting them ready, I thought it over and thought to myself, 'Well, what the hell? I may as well tell him.' We were already half way there and nothing was left for us in New York. He was out getting breakfast, so I continued getting ready. Made sure to primp a little bit more on this day as if that would help. Well, when he pulled in my heart began to jump as my stomach sank in the other direction.

"When he came inside he already knew by the look on my face that something was up. 'What is it?' he questioned as he came inside and I ran and hugged him. I gave him a kiss on those soft lips and began to grab the words out of thin air. 'Well,' I said sweetly to him, 'there's a bun in the oven.'

'What,' he said back to me, shocked as he raised those adorable bushy eyebrows.

'Jason, I'm pregnant!' I told him and he just stood there for a second as his arms dropped back to his side. I could read his body language and see the shock on his face but I figured it would wear off and he was just surprised. Oh, if I would have known then what I know now," she laughed.

"So, let me get this straight. I'm not really getting the point of where any of this says that me and you have so much in common like you say," Heather interjected.

"Just hold your horses, young 'un, I'm getting there. I just had to show you how much Jason meant to me, what Landon means to you, so that you would understand," Kareen flashed that sedating smile in Heather's direction. The two girls made a left after the long stretch of Main Street, and Tom's Corner Store came into view. "This is what we have in common, Heather," Kareen stated as she pointed to Tom's Corner Store. Heather got that empty feeling in her stomach again as she saw what had fallen into the line of sight of Kareen's finger. The two then stopped and sat on one of the old park benches that had obviously seen better days.

"Tom's?" Heather questioned to make sure she was tracking correctly with what Kareen was trying to show her.

"Yes, Tom's Heather," Kareen answered. "And this is where the puzzle pieces are going to start falling into place for you and you will see exactly what I am saying."

"When I told Jason and he tensed up, it surprised me but he seemed to mellow out towards the end of the day. We decided to stay around Quantsville for the day because he said he was in no mood to drive at the moment. I definitely understood and I was just going to support him. I was glad the weight was off my chest and he finally knew."

"Gotcha on that one, too," Heather interrupted. They looked at each other, smiled, and rocked the kid's strollers back and forth a couple times to keep them content and came to the realizations that an hour had passed and the babies were fast asleep.

"Well, I woke up the next morning and Jason was gone. He left a note on his pillow saying that he was leaving to find himself and that he would be back soon with our way out of that mess. I had no idea what his way out was going to be. I just, you know, got dressed like a normal day and waited for him there. Well, day turned into night and I began to get worried, but I couldn't do anything. He was not answering his cell phone and he had our only form of transportation with him. It's then that I saw it on the news," Kareen's voice began to fall off into the cool breeze and rustle of the tree leaves.

"Brace yourself for this one, Heather."

"Ok," Heather reluctantly responded, knowing that she was about to hear something that would hit her like a ton of bricks. It was one of those moments that you just know, and she just knew.

"Jason lost control of everything that morning, Heather. He was a good man, but he felt he was trapped and he had mouths to feed. I had never seen him hurt anyone in my life. I swear to you he was a good guy," her voice trailed off and, for the first time, Heather saw Kareen's smile disappear and tears began to run down the woman's face.

"Please continue," Heather comforted her in an effort to get her to start talking again.

"Okay, you have to know sooner or later," Kareen said through a muffled sob. The two made eye contact and Heather saw the glow replaced with the looks of a terrified child.

What could it be, she wondered. What could be this damn bad that she can't just spit it out and tell me? What could be this damn bad?

# PART 9

"Heather . . . ." Kareen began, her voice trembling. "Jason lost his mind that day. He went to a pawn shop, got a pistol, and went to Tom's Take Out just across the way. I don't know what happened after that, Heather. No one does. But my Jason and your Landon was taken from us that day."

"What the fuck?" Heather said in a more than audible tone, as an older couple flashed a scolding look in their direction.

"Heather, let me explain further," Kareen pleaded. "I know what you're thinking. I didn't realize it until that day when I ran into you at the funeral thing. When you told me that it had been exactly a year, I knew then that's why things got that way."

"Well," Heather cut her off, "first off, how do you know basically everything about my life? Like, where I live and my phone number? That's crazy!"

"Seriously, Heather?" Kareen answered. "This is a small town. How hard do you think it was to find these things out? Real crazy, huh?"

"Yeah, I guess you're right," Heather answered deflated. "Well, Where do we go from here, Kareen? I mean, why did you tell me all this? Better yet, what are you still doing in this small Kentucky town?"

"There's more to the story, just hold up. Damn, that red hair does not do your attitude justice."

"Well," Heather blushed with a small smile "I'm sorry. Go on."

"Well, when I was watching the News Channel 7 and Jason's name and what had happened came across the scroll tape and I burst into tears. I knew what he had done. Hell, he was scared. He would have three mouths to feed and no job. He was just looking for a way to give us a jump start, and he must not have remembered the trust fund my parents gave me."

"But, that does not give someone a reason to just go out on a fucking shooting rampage. You don't know, Kareen! You just don't know what it has done to this town. What it did to me and Braylen. Braylen will never know his daddy now. How do you explain that to your child as they grow?" Heather said as she was growing into a frenzy.

"Seriously, if you would stop interrupting me, girl, damn." Kareen cut Heather off this time, heated as well.

"You don't even know how crazy this all is, Kareen," Heather answered quietly. "You just expect me to be ok with you now that I know that your kid had something to do with my Landon being ripped away from me."

"Listen, Heather, before you piss me off. Just fucking listen. You're being too fucking hard headed girl. Do you want to know why I'm here or what is going on? Anything of that sort?"

Heather nodded, astonished to hear the girl raise her voice even further.

"Then shut the fuck up and listen for once then." She then continued her story. "After I got everything in my head straight and it sank in, I got the kids ready to go. We got a ride to the police station in town. I got questioned a little bit and they let me go. I then headed back to New York and took his children to their grandparents. It was hard for me, but hell I wasn't even their stepmom. I had no legal right over them. Well, as hard as it was to do, I dropped 'em off and then I just drove around for the rest of the day trying to figure out what I should do, just searching for some type of answer and then it occurred to me. Why don't I just drive back here? I liked this town and it was quite. I had lost everything I looked forward to. Tennessee and New York would remind me too much of Jason. This place, even though he died here, it's new and it's fresh. It's my halfway home, sort of. It's the little town I had set my dreams on growing old in. I never expected I would run into you. In the hospital, I had no clue and I know you didn't."

"Well, sorry for the interjection, but why did you come back here and how are you living here if it's just you and Steph? Where are you living and how are you paying for it?" Heather questioned.

"Well, good question, Heather. I knew you would be wondering that. That's what got me to tell you the story in the first place." Kareen paused and looked around. "It's called a trust fund, Heather. I lost my parents in a fire when I was 17. Turns out they were decently wealthy people and left my college fund behind for me."

Heather looked at her still not knowing what to think and questioned accordingly this time in an annoyed tone, "What does this have to do with me, Kareen? Why are you here and what do you need me for? I'm not your trust fund," she finished as she rolled her deep blue eyes.

"I'm here because, like I said, we have a lot in common. I moved back here, not trying to find you, but to start a life of my own. I had no idea that anybody was killed in that robbery except for my Jason. I didn't even know Landon existed 'till the day at that funeral."

"Yeah, and the class ring....?" Heather questioned as her voice trailed off.

"The class ring. Well, that's a different story," Kareen started. "At the hospital, you were in such a rage, twisting and turning as they were wheeling you back. I was walking down the hall to try to get the soreness out of my legs and to get bearings on what I would do. Well, you were clutching that necklace with his ring in it. You sat up and reached for your stomach and you didn't realize you had your fingers intertwined in the necklace. In that motion, you ripped it off yourself and the ring went skipping across the floor in my direction. I just knelt down and picked it up. It's not a large hospital. You know, nothing about this place is large."

"Well, that makes sense," Heather answered. "I'm sorry for freaking out about everything. I know you have to think I'm crazy by now for flipping out over all this stuff on you. I still don't understand what you want with me though or how you expect me to look at you the same."

"I don't expect you to look at me the same, Heather. I just figured we could lean on each other. I know we are in the same basic situation. Both of us are walking aimlessly around with babies under our arms and no man at our side."

"Yeah," Heather began "I was talking to my mother just yesterday that I could use a man in my life right now. My mother thought I was crazy, but you know Braylen needs a man in his life as well. Hell, you never know if me and Landon would have lasted the rest of our lives. I mean, I loved him. I still love him, but I can't keep on torturing myself like this. I just know that he will always be my son's father and a piece of me will always love him. Nothing's saying I can't love again. I know everyone would turn their back on me, though, and that's what I'm afraid of. Who would go for me even when I have a kid strapped to my side twenty four seven?"

Kareen's laughter drew Heather out of the rant. "Chill, Heather. I'm sure nobody would hold it against you for wanting a father figure in your life. Damn, girl, take a breath. I figured you would be all pissed and trying to hurt me and you're sitting here rambling about finding someone to love."

"Yeah, that's me," Heather blushed as she answered.

"Just know I understand, Heather. I really do." Kareen said as she placed her hand on Heather's leg in a way such as to comfort her. The two then stood up and grabbed the strollers. The sun was going down on that sleepy town, and it was getting chilly.

# PART 10

"So, where do we go from here?" Heather began. "I mean, what do you want to accomplish by telling me all this and getting me out here?"

"As crazy as it sounds, hun, I was sort of pacing back and forth and wondering if we could solve that lonely thing. I'd like for you to move in with me," Kareen quickly blurted. "It would make everything so much easier, I feel."

"Move in with you?" Heather choked on her coffee as she was finishing the cup. "You want me to move in with you?"

"Well, yes, Heather. I mean I know it sounds crazy, but it's not as crazy as it seems. Think about it. We are both in the same situation here and you have never been away from home. You don't want Braylen growing up thinking that grandma and grandpa are mommy and daddy. You get what I'm saying?" Kareen finished now in a more calm tone.

Damn, she had a good explanation of everything, Heather thought. She then pondered for a second as to what she should do as she paused to kick a rock on the sidewalk. "Hell, let's do it!" she blurted out. "What's the worst that could happen?"

A smile replaced the nervousness on Kareen's face and she exclaimed. "That's the spirit, girl! Exactly what could go more wrong than everything already has?" The two smiled at each other excited about the possibilities of what was coming next and continued on the walk. The subject then jumped from random gossip magazines to reality shows as the two slowly walked their way back to Kareen's car under the dim glow of streetlights.

Heather felt like she had somehow just made friends with the enemy, but inside she knew she just couldn't blame Kareen for the death of Landon. It would be hard to completely trust this girl, though. She was a city girl and a stranger, but it was impossible to argue with her. Hell, with it, she thought as she cranked up the stereo in the car a few notches.

"You like this song?" Kareen interrupted Heather's train of thought. "Yeah, I tend to like everything they put on this station and actually music helps keep Braylen knocked out."

"Really now?" Kareen questioned. "That's the same thing with Steph. You play some old country or classic rock and she is out like a light." The two then began to sing along with Tom Petty's "Free Fallin" and they continued the duet all the way to Heather's house accompanied by smiles and laughter the whole way. Two lost souls had just connected through the most unlikely of paths and they both knew the world was looking up. Heather's drive way came into view and Kareen whipped the car into the drive. "I'll call you tomorrow," Kareen blurted to Heather as she was pulling Braylen out of the back seat. "We can figure out the details then."

\* \* \*

Heather knew this was going to be a rough conversation with her parents, she thought as she was walking up the drive. She would talk to them tomorrow and deal with all the drama then, but she was excited for what was going to happen. She was excited for the change that was coming for her and Braylen. She felt this could be a new fresh chapter in her life in which everything would go right for once. She also felt crazy at the same time, however. She had no idea where Kareen lived or what type of place she had. She remembered Kareen saying something about a trust fund, but hell, how much money could she possibly have in the trust fund. She knew that things would be rough, and she knew that this would shock everybody in town. No one knew who Kareen was. Hell, Heather knew herself that Kareen was pretty much a stranger. But something about that girl just made her feel at home with everything. She just had that commanding presence that everything was going to be alright with her around. And Kareen had the guts to tell Heather straight up exactly what had happened. That takes a lot of courage. By this time in her thoughts, she had made it inside the house and laid Braylen down in his crib. She was thankful he was finally sleeping in it, so she could have her bed alone. She was scared to death when he first came home that she would roll over on him in her sleep. "Goodnight," she whispered as she kissed Braylen on the head and walked into her room to lie down and sleep. She sure was excited, she thought as she drifted off to sleep.

\* \* \*

"You want to do what?" Heather's mother shouted as Heather threw the new twist on her mother. "Just yesterday you said you didn't even have a good feeling about the girl."

"Yes, mother, I know, "Heather interrupted Lisa before she could go any farther. "We had a long talk last night and I got her back story. You know? Where she's from and things like that. We are pretty much the same people, you know. Kareen's man was killed in a coal mine accident. She moved here off the settlement she got. So both our babies are without fathers. It just seems right," Heather blatantly lied to her mother. She knew that her mother would never accept the truth in the way she had. Hell, she thought, it's none of her business anyways. I'm nineteen and I can do whatever I want with my child.

"I don't like this one bit, Heather Mae," Lisa yanked Heather right out of her thoughts. "How do you plan on paying for everything? Do you even know where she lives? Are you fucking high?"

Heather stood up from the table and walked back to her room. She paused turned around and looked at her mother about halfway across the dining room and gave her one brief blurt, "Fuck it. We can talk about it later."

Who is this monster, Lisa thought as she brushed a tear from her eye. She felt as if she had lost her daughter.

\* \* \*

Heather threw on some faded jeans and one of Landon's hoodies, went to the bathroom and brushed her teeth, and then went and got Braylen from her father.

"What was that about, hunny?" her father questioned.

"Oh, nothing," Heather said as she flashed that familiar innocent little girl smile in his direction. "Mom's just overreacting about something as always."

"It seemed like it was more than that," her father responded.

"Dad, really, it's fine," she stated as she grabbed Braylen from him and walked briskly out the door. She grabbed Braylen's stroller out of the trunk of her car and buckled him in snuggly, covering him up with a blanket, as it was a breezy day, and started on the normal lap around town. She walked this lap every day. It was her way of losing the baby weight and it gave her some fresh air. The first few times were rough, however, as everyone wanted to stop her and look at the town's new hero. She just continued on her normal route and began to get lost in her thoughts. She couldn't help but smiling when the thought of Kareen and their new journey slide into her mind.

"You and me going fishing in the dark." The country ringtone from her phone began to play that familiar tune and she was startled out of her deep thoughts. It was Kareen. Heather fumbled around with the phone as she hurriedly picked it up and answered.

"Whatcha doin', girl?" Kareen's prissy voice questioned.

"Oh, just walking around town, trying to finish off the rest of this baby weight and just be alone with my thoughts," Heather answered.

"Well, I'm sorry to interrupt. I was just wondering if you and Braylen would like to join me and Steph for dinner tonight at my place." Kareen questioned.

"Well, sure. I think we would love that. I'd like to see my new home anyways. I threw the idea on my mother today, and that didn't go so well."

"Oh, no," Kareen cut her off in a concerned tone.

"It's ok, Kareen. She just doesn't understand. We can talk about it tonight."

"Ok, sounds like a plan," Kareen answered. "How does 7:30pm sound?"

"Sounds like what time Imma see you in my driveway," Heather responded in a playful tone.

"I'll see you then, hun."

Heather hung up and couldn't help but noticing just how perfect everything about this idea was beginning to seem. She continued on her walk around town singing merrily along the way. Once back at home she rushed to her room and searched for something to wear. Wow! Been awhile since I've done this, she thought as she threw clothes combinations out on her messy bed.

* * *

Sure enough, at 7:30, she heard the familiar VW horn give off it's just short of mighty beep. She skipped out of the house, not bothering with telling her parents where she was going this time. She made it to the car, buckled Braylen in the back seat, and talked to Steph a few seconds as the girl rambled off some chuckles and other babbly sounds. The two kids were starting to blurt out words here and there, so Heather made sure to listen extra close for words that sounded something like 'mommy' when Braylen spoke. "You two are just," she whispered as she shut the door. She then hopped in the passenger seat noticing that Kareen took extra care of herself that day as well.

"You look good, girl," Kareen exclaimed with a shiny white smile.

"Yeah? You look good yourself, momma," Heather playfully replied. "Take me to your castle," she followed with a laugh.

"You got it" Kareen exclaimed as she pulled out of the drive and pressed the accelerator on the little car.

# PART 11

Heather couldn't help but feel the now normal wave of excitement rush over her as her house disappeared in the mirror. It was a warm day so they drove with the radio up and the windows down. Once again, they sang every song that came on the radio as the babies in the back seat squealed with laughter at what they were witnessing. The air of a new beginning was on them all and they could feel it as if it were a quilted comforter on a cold winter day. It was warm and it was welcome and, as the miles stretched on, Heather felt a sense of being carefree for the first time in a long time. The wind in her hair felt revitalizing and she had someone there that actually understood. It truly was a good day she thought. The sky was cast with the sun's falling and it looked as if God had painted it patiently with an easel and pastels. She was relaxed and ready for the journey that had been cast upon her. She no longer felt as if she were trapped. Kareen just seemed to give off an air of control and a sense of 'everything was going to be alright' with her around. Everything was going to be ok, she thought, and she was happy.

"So, what you wanna eat?" Kareen playfully questioned.

"I, um . . . . I don't know," Heather stuttered as she hadn't even given thought.

"Well, I got lasagna in the oven," Kareen chuckled. "Just thought I would be half polite and ask."

"Yeah, well, that was mighty nice of you," Heather replied as she pushed her hand out the window into the wind, moving it up and down, cutting it like some sort of fake jet through the air. "So where do you live, Kareen? Where are you taking me in this chariot of yours?" Heather questioned.

"It's just up around the bend. I picked a house out in the country with a big yard for when Steph got a little older. A lot of the trust fund has gone into it, but I figured if it was paid off in cash that would be a big step and one less thing to worry about."

"Yes, definitely," Heather replied. It can't be much of a house if it's paid for in cash, she thought to herself. I wonder if this is as good idea as I thought. Her thoughts were replaced as a large house began to take shape up the driveway the car was swallowing.

Well, I've been wrong before, Heather thought to herself as the house split the trees as the main view from her perspective. It was a beautiful place and she wondered how she never knew it was there. She had been down that road thousands of times, just not up that drive she thought. The grass was fresh and tidy in the fenced-in yard. It was brick, and the second story was tan vinyl siding. A nice country house with a garage and a bay window in the front.

"Wow!" The words slipped out of her mouth before she could fight them back.

"Yeah," Kareen said as she put the car in park. "Welcome to your new home. It's not so bad on the inside. I'm sure you will feel right at home in no time."

Heather just looked at the house in front of her, stunned that she was so wrong. Damn, she thought to herself, I don't think much else could go right lately. This place was just too much for a first house. She had a stunned look on her face as she fumbled for the door latch to get Braylen out of the back.

"Well, let me give you the grand tour," Kareen said as she pulled Steph out of her car seat. "Of course, this is the yard. See what I mean? It's the perfect size to have some kids run around in. And we could just sit on the porch swing and watch them grow."

"Yeah, it's a beautiful yard. Who does your yard work?" Heather asked.

"Well, me of course, silly. You have your walks around town, I have my yard work. It's not so bad and it's what I always dreamed of. When I was in New York, we didn't have a back yard. That place was a concrete playground. This one is so much better for kids."

They then turned and started to walk up the cobblestone driveway which was accented in marigolds and lilies on both sides. Not bad for a city girl, Heather thought to herself as she made her way up onto the wraparound porch.

"Let's go inside. Get that crazy stunned look off your face," Kareen poked in Heather's direction.

"This place is pretty incredible for you to pay for on your own," Heather answered.

"Two words, Heather: Trust. Fund." Kareen still had the inviting smile on her face as she opened the door.

The doorway opened into a beautiful open layout floor plan. The floor in the main walk was hardwood. And beautiful hardwood, Heather thought to herself. She got lost in the beauty as she began to take off her shoes.

"Cute socks," Kareen laughed as she watched Heather take off her shoes.

"I always mismatch the color of my socks," Heather answered. "Just something I've done since I was little."

"Well, it's cute," Kareen continued to laugh. "I think the lasagna is about done, so we will eat first and I will give you the grand tour second."

"Sounds like a plan," Heather answered as she sat Braylen on the ground. He was beginning to get around pretty well and Steph was as well. They walked into the kitchen and it just happened to take Heather by surprise as well. The floor was a beaming grey tile and all the appliances were stainless steel. It had an odd shaped ceiling fan in the middle over the island. The curtains were a perfect burgundy accent. "Wow, my mother would love this kitchen," Heather expressed her approval.

"Yeah, it was a main selling point for me. I love to cook so I had to have a nice kitchen."

Heather and Kareen then walked into the dining room. It was brightly lit with a chandelier in the middle and followed the hardwood and burgundy theme. Heather felt as if she was going to wake up from the dream at any minute. This couldn't be the place where she would call home. It just couldn't.

"You know, it's so easy to tell by the look on your face when you are getting lost in your thoughts," Kareen said as she sat the food on the table.

"Sorry," Heather apologized, "this just all seems like a dream."

"Well, it's not crazy, so let's sit down and enjoy a meal. Tell me how things went with your mother."

"Well, it didn't go so well," Heather began. "She flipped out about how I barely know you, so I got a little heated as well. I lied to her and told her that Jason was a coal miner and died in the mines. She doesn't know you're from New York or anything about you, that I know, so we should keep that between us for now. You know what I'm saying, hun?"

"Yeah, it's probably best that people don't know about the connection we have with each other. It is pretty crazy for us to have met in the way we did. One thing about these small towns, Heather, is everybody seems to find out about everything, huh?" Kareen asked.

"Yeah, everybody knows everything about everything in these small parts. Hell, by tomorrow everyone will know that I'm moving in with the new random girl in town. Everyone will say how crazy I am because I barely know you. But, you know, it feels like I've known you forever. It's crazy."

"It's not so crazy, Heather," Kareen answered. "People just don't know the real connection we have and the crazy amount we have in common."

"That's for sure," Heather finished Kareen's thoughts.

They then turned to the food and the conversation was focused on lighter things. The babies managed to wobble into the room and gave Kareen and Heather something else to talk about for a little while. It would be good for the two to grow up together, Heather thought as she watched the two.

"Well, I see you were a good girl and finished your plate," Kareen joked. "Would you like the grand tour?"

"Sure would. Show me the rest of this palace," Heather responded.

Kareen stood up and walked over to Heather and grabbed her by the hand as she flashed that familiar bright smile. "Come on," she said quickly and they began the tour. It was a 4 bedroom, 2 and a half bath house. It had a dining room, living room, and den beyond the regular amenities. Heather was excited to see the books in the den as she was a reader herself. She was glad they would at least have this in common compared to all the tragic similarities. This one was actually inviting. The two then made their way upstairs and walked across the balcony to view the rooms.

"This is my room and down the hall is . . . ." Kareen was cut off as Heather and her collided. Heather had gotten lost in the view from the balcony.

"I, uh," Heater began to apologize, but was cut off by Kareen's deep stare. Heather stared into Kareen's eyes for what seemed an eternity and felt herself being pushed up against the wall.

Kareen then brushed the hair from Heather's eyes and whispered, "You're so beautiful." Heather's mind was rushing, but soon she wasn't able to think at all as the thoughts were replaced by a deep kiss. Kareen then gave her a brief smile and began to walk to the other room.

# PART 12

"Kareen, what was that?" Heather asked.

"That was my bedroom, hun," Kareen responded, trying to brush away the question.

"No . . . The kiss. What was that?" Heather questioned.

"Oh, Heather, you were asking for it," Kareen responded with a smile. Heather just stared dumbfounded. She wondered if she really had been asking for it. She had never experienced something like that and the way it replayed in her head did seem like something that you would see in a movie; something that happens to everyone else in the big cities, not in that small town. She had never even heard of anyone except for the "freaks" being attracted to the same sex. The thing that made her the most dumbfounded, however, is that she kissed back. She went with it and she realized that she had put her arm around Kareen as they were kissing. What the hell is that? Where did it come from? This isn't me. The thoughts all rushed through her head. She had no idea how to grasp any of the feelings she had inside, but she didn't need to. Kareen dragged her out of her thoughts as she grabbed her hand.

"Sorry, Heather," Kareen explained. "You just looked inviting. Good kisser, though."

The smile never left Kareen's face as she showed Heather through the rest of the house. She just kept beaming as if she were a child that had just gotten everything it wanted for Christmas. Heather, however, was a wreck. She knew she wanted a new relationship, but she wondered what this moving in together thing would really mean. Did Kareen like her, as in "like her," or was that just one of those crazy moments in life where you go with it? She didn't know and as surprising as it is, didn't really care. She was just going with it, so she joined in on the smiling, too. She was still excited to call this home, and, damn, she thought to herself, I've never been touched that gently or kissed that deeply in my life. It was as if she knew everything about what I loved and threw it all at me in one moment.

"Guess I can't blame the lesbians now," she accidently spoke aloud as she was getting lost in her thoughts.

"What?" Kareen questioned with a grin. "Girl, it was just a kiss, not like we fucked or anything."

The tour was over and Heather thoroughly approved of the house. They then went and found the kids. Braylen and Steph were still happy go lucky wandering around in the child-proof den. Hell, this was safer than her own home, Heather thought to herself. They then snatched up their respective children and Heather followed Kareen into the nursery. Heather was stunned as Kareen already had an extra crib in there. Kareen caught the look on Heather's face and gave a simple explanation.

"When I left to come here, I knew there was a chance I would have twins, so I brought Jason's kids' cribs as well. The grandparents didn't take everything I had, so it was easy enough to just bring what I felt I needed. I know you have your own, but I think it would work for tonight."

"Tonight?" Heather questioned.

"Yeah. I figured you would just stay the night since its already late, hun," Kareen began to explain. "We can talk about everything and how we are going to work things out. With us living together and all, we can probably both carry part-time jobs now and babysit each other's child. I think it would be a huge bonus, you know, with all the freedom and such."

"Yeah I'll stay," Heather gave a quick uncomfortable response. Kareen didn't bother to question the uncomfortable tone, but she just gave her usual wide perfect smile. Kareen knew what she had done to Heather, but she liked it. She thought from the second she saw Heather that she was beautiful, but she didn't really expect the kiss. She had done the normal college drunk kisses with girls, but nothing serious. She was surprised as well, but unlike Heather she was good at hiding things and she was also surprised at how good the kiss was. Maybe it was the fact that neither of them had had anyone to love since the children's' dads had died. That coulda been it, she thought to herself. Whatever it was, she wasn't going to let Heather know it surprised her. She liked having the control and she felt she could use it to her advantage, and, hell, nothing's wrong with a little secret now and then. She loved how Heather's arm had felt around her waist. Loved it so much in fact that it scared her.

"Where's your diapers?" Heather asked. She could see that Kareen was lost in some sort of thought and this was a first. She wondered what the hell Kareen could be thinking so deeply about. It wasn't that kiss was it? That couldn't mess with her as much as it messes with me, Heather continued in her thoughts. She's a city girl; she has to have some sort of experience with that type of thing. She was clueless, however, at how big any of it really was.

"They are in the closet," Kareen responded. "Why don't you grab me one as well?"

"Sure thing, hun," Heather said with a smile. She went to the closet and grabbed out a couple diapers and some wipes. "Crazy how fast they grow," Heather made conversation as she was searching for the powder.

"Yeah," Kareen began, "they grow way too damn fast. Now that Steph and Braylen are walking, it's really going to start getting hectic for us. We will chase these rascals everywhere and they will be squealing with laughter the whole way," she finished.

"Yeah, this is all pretty new to me," Heather admitted as the two laid the babies back into their cribs. They then walked into the living room.

"Pick a movie and I'll go pop some popcorn," Kareen offered.

"Sure thing," Heather said with a smile. She walked into the living room and found her way to the movie cabinet. She saw everything in there. "How the hell am I to pick one when there are three hundred to choose from?" she whispered to herself. She went ahead and picked up "The Notebook." She loved that movie and figured any girl loved it, so it would work for the night. Hell, half the titles in there she had never seen and a boring movie on a night like this would just make things awkward.

"Good choice," Kareen said as she walked into the room carrying two separate bowls of popcorn.

"Yeah, I figured every girl loves this movie," Heather explained. "You know, I really know nothing about you, so I had to take a shot in the dark on this one."

"Yeah, I plan to change that not knowing anything about each other nonsense" Kareen said with a laugh. "Hell, with kisses like that, I'm interested in knowing every little detail." Heather didn't answer. She just sat and wished she had some sort of clue what Kareen meant by "every detail."

The rest of the night was spent talking about specifics of everything and getting the back story on each other past the dreaded deaths of their significant others. Heather was set to begin moving in the next day and figured she could get everything moved in within a day. She didn't really have much to move except for Braylen's crib and clothes. She just wondered how her dad was going to take this. She felt he wouldn't be comfortable with his baby moving out with his grandson, but she knew this was a step she had to take.

"Well, I'm going to sleep." Kareen said as the credits began to roll. "I'll see you in the morning, hun. I wish you knew how excited I am for this journey we are starting."

"Yeah, see you in the morning, crazy," Heather said with a shy smile. She hadn't used that smile since she used to tease Landon when he wanted to get in her pants. Both caught the smile and Kareen just put her hand on her hip, gave the smile right back, and then walked up stairs to her bed room.

# PART 13

Heather then found her way upstairs and into her room. She stripped down to the bra and underwear, since that's all she had around. She then walked down the hall to check on the babies before she found her way to bed. Braylen and Steph were both sound asleep and peaceful as angels in their crib. Heather stood there for a few moments and watched them sleep and her mind began to wonder back to the kiss earlier that day. She wondered if, since she didn't pull away, if it would be something that happened more often. She also wondered why the hell she flashed Kareen that "I want you smile." She hadn't used that one in forever and it shocked her that it just brought itself to the surface on its own. Was her body trying to tell her something? Was it possible that she could, herself, be bisexual? No, that's gross, she thought to herself with a grimace. I could never be something like that. It was just a fluke. She was satisfied with the conclusion she had come to, so she wandered on down the hall back to the room.

She found her way to the big bed in the middle of the room. It had a fluffy white comforter, but the rest of the room was pretty bare. It was almost as if Kareen had already prepared for her. She drifted off to sleep wondering what type of madness the future held in store.

* * *

She awoke the next morning to the smell of bacon and pancakes. She whisked her hair back in a pony tail, checked on the still sound asleep babies, and slowly walked down the stairs as she rubbed the tired out of her eyes.

"Well, that's a hell of a look to walk around the house in," Kareen shot to her as she reached the last step. Heather then realized that she was still in her bra and underwear.

"I, uh . . . ." Heather began to explain, but no words came. She simply blushed and continued her walk to the kitchen. Hell, she thought to herself if this girl wants me to move in, she may as well see everything anyways; she's bound to in the future. She found her way to the kitchen and discovered that her nose was right. Kareen was almost done finishing up the pancakes and the bacon was in the stainless steel microwave. Perfect, Heather thought to herself. At least the woman can cook.

"If you need to borrow anything, Heather, I have plenty of clothes," Kareen offered. "That is a pretty sexy set you're wearing there, though. No wonder you shot me that playful kiss last night," she finished with a playful smile.

Heather remembered the kiss, but she had woken up wondering if it was just a crazy dream from sleeping in a foreign bed. She found her answer, however, and simply managed to let her face turn an even deeper shade of red as she grabbed the pancakes and took them to the dining room. Kareen followed with the bacon and a pitcher of orange juice. The two sat down and enjoyed the meal that Kareen had prepared. The conversation ranged from various topics, but the main was how Heather was going to explain to her mother that she was moving out so soon.

"I guess we will just have to see how she takes it," Heather explained as the two stood up to return the dirty dishes to the sink. "I don't think she will yell in front of you, but who knows?"

"You're turning twenty in a month, Heather," Kareen tried to give her some comfort. "Kids don't stay at home forever."

The two went upstairs and got the kids ready to leave. They were their usually happy selves just babbling along and that made Heather's day brighter. She hated what she knew Kareen would see at her house. She knew that both her parents would overreact. Maybe she should tell them about the kiss, she thought as she laughed. They would just love to hear this. She gathered up Braylen's diaper bag, and then realized what she was doing. She unpacked everything she had packed and then repacked it for a trip. She would return there that night. This was her home, she thought, I wonder when it will sink in.

"Let's go, crazy," Kareen called from downstairs. "Leave that jacket off; it's a beautiful day outside." She further explained. Heather threw the jacket in the center of the Fluffy, now unkempt, bed, grabbed Braylen, and headed down the carpeted steps and out the front door.

"Let's go get my stuff," she playfully shot at Kareen. "Time to make my mother have an aneurism," she laughed as she climbed in the car and they pulled off.

\* \* \*

"You're doing what, Heather?" Lisa questioned as if she couldn't believe what she had heard. "How are you going to pay for everything? You don't even know this girl, or anything about her." Heather knew it was going to be like this so she tried to calm her mother.

"We talked about everything, mom. We're going to live off her trust fund until . . ."

Kareen cut her off and began to explain to Lisa, "My parents died when I was 17. They left me a pretty substantial amount of money, Lisa. Heather will be just fine there with me. We can get jobs and use each other as babysitters. Heather can't stay here forever, you know."

Lisa was good with the girl's explanation until she heard the last line Kareen had voiced. How dare this random fluesy tell her what is good for her girl? "Heather can stay here however the hell long she wants to stay here," Lisa shot in both Kareen and Heather's direction.

"Mom," Heather began, "we talked it all out last night. It's a done deal. It is just ten minutes down the road."

"You're welcome to come out anytime you wish for a visit or to stay," Kareen added desperately trying to de escalate the situation. It was to no avail, however, and Lisa stormed out of the room leaving Kareen, the two babies, and Heather there to pack.

Heather packed clothes into two suitcases while Kareen kept the babies busy. She knew she wouldn't get everything in one trip, but at the moment she didn't care. She just wanted to get what she needed and get out of the place before her father returned home from work.

"I can tell you just got out of high school," Kareen joked as she twirled a cheerleading ribbon around her finger.

"Yeah, seems like just yesterday I was in high school. Life just happens so fast, you know. When your little, you hear the old people talk about the younger days. Well, I feel like that now," she paused with a chuckle that quickly disappeared. "I miss everything about those days, you know. Having someone to hold on to. Not worrying about a thing in this world. Nothing at all, except for me and Landon." She abruptly stopped the rant as she had realized the name that slithered out of her mouth. Almost two years now and finally it didn't absolutely kill her to say his name.

"Yea," Kareen added, "it will probably always feel like just yesterday, but we have each other now. So, let's just go with that," she flashed a smile in Heather's direction as Heather began to put all the boxes and suitcases together in the middle of the floor. "Smile for me sunshine." Heather looked up and managed a small smile.

"M-M-A-M-M-A!" Mama stumbled out of Braylen's mouth as he walked towards Heather. She then snatched him up and began to tickle him. He finally said it, she thought to herself as she stood up. Finally, my baby boy said it. Kareen gave Heather a hug because she sensed the excitement.

"Oh, no," Kareen joked. "You sure your head is going to fit out that door now?"

"Shut up," Heather shot back. "Let's get out of here," she finished, grabbed both girls, grabbed a handful of things, and walked to the car.

\* \* \*

"Ah, this looks much better," Heather sighed in relief as she finished putting everything she brought to the room away.

"I'd say," Kareen answered as she poked her head in the doorway. "I had no clue what I was going to do with this room. The furniture was left in here from the last owners."

"I wondered why in the world you had two beds already," Heather commented.

"Looks like it turned out for the best, though," Kareen said as she began to walk towards Heather. Before Heather knew it, it was a replay of yesterday. She felt Kareen's hands squeeze her hips as they pulled her close, forehead touching forehead. With a little kiss, Kareen pushed Heather back on the bed following every inch. "I wish you knew how beautiful you are when you're in deep thought," Kareen began to speak, but Heather reached out, cradled her hand around Kareen's neck, and shut her up with the passion of a deep kiss. Heather's mind was going spastic now. It felt so right, but it felt so wrong.

"Stop," the words blurted out of Heather's mouth as Kareen began to slither her tongue slowly down Heather's neck.

"What?" Kareen responded more in a breath than an audible tone.

# PART 14

"Kareen, seriously, stop," Heather said in a desperate tone as she pushed Kareen away. "We can't keep doing this. I don t know what you have done in your past, but this is seriously not me. It wouldn't be good for the kids either."

"I'm sorry," Kareen explained, "I have never done anything like this either. I just got lost in the moment and, besides, you're the one that reached up and pulled me to you. This isn't entirely my fault."

"I know, I know. It just can't be right," Heather added. The two stood up and Kareen turned and walked out of the room.

"I'll go start on some dinner," she yelled back to Heather as she started to walk down the stairs. What the hell is going on with me, Heather thought to herself. She knew that that one wasn't a fluke. It wasn't entirely Kareen's fault either. She had pulled the girl closer to her and she was actually comfortable in those moments. She wondered if she really could have that side of her that was attracted to another woman and, if so, what would she do with it. They couldn't raise two kids in that small town as lesbians. It would destroy the kids' chance at being anything because they would be judged on their mothers' actions. "Oh, well," she whispered as she finished her thoughts and walked downstairs to help with dinner.

*   *   *

The next three weeks went without incident and Heather began to get suited in her new home very well. She also started taking online courses through a grant which had been set up for single mothers. She thought phlebotomy was a good choice because she could get her specialized courses done through the local high school's technical center. She knew the teachers there, so it would be easy and she could get a job at the hospital. Half the old ladies there were bound to die off sometime soon anyways, she thought, so job openings would show. Kareen started the program as well.

It made Heather uncomfortable at first that Kareen followed so closely in her footsteps, but once again Kareen explained herself and Heather couldn't help but feel comfortable with Kareen's explanation. Heather knew it would be good to have someone to go to class with and to study with anyways. All her friends were off at a real college partying and doing what she had, three weeks earlier, but with a bottle in hand. She no longer envied them for that and she was happy where she was. She had somewhat of a family now with her, Kareen, and the kids. Her parents had somewhat come around and made a visit every Sunday to eat dinner. Heather's dad fell in love with Kareen's cooking, much to Lisa's dismay.

She knew today would be a real test, however, as it was the children's second birthday party and she didn't really know who was going to show or how it would all play out. Outside of Heather's immediate family, no one really knew where Heather was living, so today would be the day when everyone figured it out. Kareen's grandparents had actually flown in for the party just the day prior, so Heather and Kareen were sharing a room for the time being. Heather couldn't help but wonder every time they locked eyes if a kiss was about to be delivered. It never happened, though, and for that Heather was glad. She didn't know if she wanted to go through the awkward moments again. She did miss the touch, though. She wondered if that was natural or if it was really something. She recounted these things in her head an average of once a week now. It was bound to happen today, she thought to herself, as she climbed out of bed and left Kareen lying there. She knew she should be prepared for anything on this day.

Kareen's grandmother was already downstairs cooking breakfast and greeted Heather with an icy glass of orange juice. Kareen's grandmother was told a completly fabricated story as well about how Jason died and how Kareen knew Heather. Kareen never told anyone what really happened to Jason. She didn't want his name to go down like that. She wanted everyone to remember him for who he was. She told them all that he was hit by a car while he was changing a blown out tire on the side of the road. It was a crazy, fabricated story and that's what made everyone bite.

"So, tell me more about you, Heather," Kareen's grandmother asked as she laid the normal bacon and two steaming chocolate chip pancakes in front of Heather. It was a meal that had become mainstay in Heather's daily diet and a perfect way to start any day.

"Well, what would you like to know Mrs. Jones?" Heather sweetly replied trying to hide that she had no clue as what to tell the woman or what Kareen had already lied to her about.

"Well, Kareen only told us that you were a good friend in high school, so I need to know basically everything if you're going to live with my baby," Mrs. Jones gave her a playful elderly smile as she invited Heather to explain the details.

"I told you everything about her, Grams," Kareen spoke up for Heather as she skipped down the steps. Her dark brown hair was straightened and the light brown eyes sparkled in the morning sun shining in through the large oak front door windows.

"Oh, I know, but I wanted to hear it from her," Mrs. Jones answered. "There could be some things that even you don't know."

"Grams, can we just eat breakfast? We need to get things ready before people start to show up," Kareen pleaded with her grandmother.

"Well, alright," Mrs. Jones finished with the same smile. Heather was glad Kareen had saved her from the barrage of questions that would have arrived if Heather had opened her mouth. She was really clueless about New York. She couldn't have answered questions about street names or stores or anything, for that matter. All she knew was Times Square and that was from watching the ball drop on TV on New Year's. Mrs. Jones left it alone for the time being and Heather was glad. Kareen really seemed to step in at the moments when she really needed a lifeline. They finished eating and then woke up the babies and got them ready for the day.

The guests started to show around noon and each showed satisfaction in where Heather had chose to live. Oddly enough, none of them questioned who Kareen was. Heather wondered if her parents had already given an explanation as to who the stranger their beloved daughter had been holding the long term sleepover with. Everyone in that small town knew each other, so they had to have asked someone questions already. At least, this is what Heather had hoped for. The most strenuous task that day was keeping Mrs. Thomas away from Heather's parents. She figured that Mrs. Thomas would want to know what made the Watersons leave glorious New York and live in the boring small town. Heather knew if that happened that everything would fall apart. Stories would get criss-crossed and Kareen and herself would look like a couple of jackasses standing there stuttering, grasping desperately for answers. Kareen managed to keep her grandmother on the porch swing which was a miracle. As the day grew longer the guests, one by one, started to leave. Aunts and Uncles each promised a return and Heather's younger teenage cousins questioned her as to why they didn't know of where Heather was staying. Each wanted to be invited out again and Kareen promised them, before Heather could answer, that they were welcome to a sleepover at any time.

"Well, that one was close," Kareen whispered to Heather as they laid the worn out toddlers down for sleep.

"Yeah," Heather responded. "I don't know how, but that actually all worked out." Both girls walked downstairs and started going through the normal ritual of a movie before sleep. It was their way of matching up each other's day and just touching base before they went to sleep. The last three weeks, the two had learned almost the entirety of each other's history on God's earth.

"Why don't we share some wine tonight instead of popcorn?" Kareen offered.

"Yeah, that sounds like a plan. You may not want to be contributing to a minor, though," Heather joked and sure enough Kareen came out with a bottle of strawberry wine and two glasses.

"With a day like today I figured this would be just a perfect way to end our night," Kareen explained.

"Oh, crazy, I don't need any explanation just turn on the TV and pour me my wine," Heather joked. The movie was a comedy and, whether it was the wine or the movie, Heather felt loopy. Might want to call it a night, she thought to herself. Three weeks without any awkward moments, I better not create another.

# PART 15

The following year flew by. A few incidents between the two females were few and far between. They knew they had to do the right thing for the children, but the desire still churned in both. They grew to have a connection as well as the children. Steph and Braylen got along really well and both were really smart toddlers. It was somewhat of a challenge for two single mothers, but together Kareen and Heather made things work; they really had no other choice. Both were doing well in college, but decided to quit because a new opportunity had arose that would take up the majority of their free time. The lease on Tom's Take Out was up and after the incident three years prior his wife had made him swear he would not sign up for another lease. Besides, old Tom had started having trouble with walking and the daily inventory itself had become a strenuous task. He was already collecting a retired Lieutenant Colonel retirement. His time with the small store was up and it was the girls' turn to try their hand at the small market.

The decision had been made over dinner a few weeks prior. Heather was strictly against it at the time, due to that being the last place her Landon took his last breath.

"You want to do what?" she blasted in Kareen's direction when she first brought it up.

"Heather, this trust fund won't last forever. I know the place holds a different meaning for you, but you may want to look past that. Hell, you never know, it may help the pain you still feel inside."

Heather knew the argument was over before it even began. Kareen was always the one that could kill all her anger with a simple brief explanation. She called up Elizabeth that night and discussed it with her. Elizabeth was hesitant as well, but explained to Heather that she needed to do something to get on her own feet. Heather and Braylen couldn't live off of Kareen forever. Elizabeth further explained to Heather that she thought that Heather at least owed Kareen something for taking her into her home and letting her stay for free. Elizabeth offered to help set up the store as well. "I'll think about it over night," was the last thing Heather said to Kareen that day. She didn't feel right about it after the twenty-four hour grace period, but reluctantly agreed.

After Tom's lease had been up, Kareen bought the store outright and put it in joint possession. She explained to Heather that she felt she owed it to her because of the help. Heather felt the part ownership was just binding her to the small town, but she knew it would at least be a guaranteed income for awhile. She had gotten over the idea of moving away, in a sense. Everything her and Braylen knew was in that small town. Family, a good school, and a good football team for him to play on. She saw the dreams of moving away grow more distant into the future to just a shimmering glimmer of hope. Kareen wanted to close the store for three weeks to do some remodeling.

"Heather, honestly, I've got forty-five thousand dollars left from the trust fund. I say we put thirty of it into the store to expand it some. Get bigger fuel tanks, update the pumps, and update the inside. I would like to update the outside, but keep its original old time look. We could even squeeze a small diner inside. Maybe four tables for the elderly after church." Knowing Kareen had a plan made her feel easier with the whole idea. If it was updated and changed inside it wouldn't remind her of Landon so much.

Three days after the transitioning of ownership, the girls began work. They hired a contractor to redo the inside and put a commercial stove in for the diner. It was Kareen's plan to run the diner while Heather ran the cash register. The floors would be polished hard wood, as well as the counter and cabinets. Kareen really like the old fashioned cabin look and Heather agreed that it did look pretty amazing. At this point she had come around and really liked the idea of the store and the opportunities it would hold. She was no longer an underage, unwed mother that no guy would like. The store would be an opportunity to meet people traveling through the small town for gas. It was another new beginning and Heather liked new beginnings. She liked the fresh start of Kareen and everything the girl had brought into Heather's life. She truly owed Kareen everything, as Elizabeth had said, so Heather worked really hard to help the construction workers with anything she could. All she really managed to do was drool and try not to get caught staring. Kareen had the same problem, only she had been lost in her stares at Heather.

Kareen had developed more than a crush on Heather. She longed for the sweet kisses she experienced a year ago, but she knew that she wasn't welcome. She knew that she would freak Heather out with such a strong come on, but she had a plan. The store was her plan on keeping Heather around for the long haul. She loved to watch Heather as she would work on getting things just in place or as Heather stared at the sweaty construction workers. Heather was amazing in that tank top and cut off shorts. She felt that if Heather had part ownership of the store, she would be stuck there with Kareen for the long run. The kids could grow up together and eventually she would talk Heather into believing the chemistry between them was ok and that the kids would understand. She had talked Jason into falling in love with her. A barely legal, blue eyed, red headed girl shouldn't be a hard task. She had plans and so far they were working. Heather was stuck now, right where Kareen wanted her. Now all she had to do was wait and the awkwardness would eventually disappear after every snuck in kiss. She had her Jason; she would have her Heather, too.

\* \* \*

It was just opening day and the girls woke up extra early that day to make sure everything was in place. They dropped the kids off at Heather's parents and made their way to the store. Heather's parents were excited for the girls' new beginning. Hell, the whole town was. To everyone it was just fitting that Tom's stay open and that it got a fresh new young set of owners. They had renamed it Tom Cats to keep the familiarity of the old store and it just seemed to fit for the couple. They continued on the drive to the store down Main Street and as always Kareen thought Heather looked beautiful as she was staring out the passenger window at the scenery going past. It was hard to hide her crush, but for the time being she had to. They made it to the store after singing every song on the radio, as always, and Heather jumped out in excitement.

"Let me get the door for you, miss," Heather said in a bright smile. Kareen walked in and to the back of the store.

"I'll fire up the grill while you do the final inventory Heather," she said as she turned the corner around the old fashioned counter.

"One hour until we open shop, girl," Heather said with a beaming smile. Kareen could only smile in return.

The hour went by fast and Heather flipped the sign on the door to say "open." They kept the placard on the door instead of going with one of the new neon signs because it held character in the little shop. Customers were in and out that day and the diner was always steady. The Coleman fish sandwich with chips were a hit for the older crowd and the younger children loved the hand dipped ice cream. That was also one of Kareen's ideas for keeping in tradition with the old time atmosphere of the place. They made more than the predicted quota for the day and both were excited for the future. Heather truly enjoyed talking to the townspeople as well as the out of town people that day while she was ringing up the gas and other various things. Thoughts swirled in her head of expansions they could do for a bar and grill in the abandoned storage part in the back, but she knew she was getting way ahead of herself. She shot a smile to Kareen as she came around the counter to change the placard back to "closed." The first day was definitely a success and Heather was pleased that she had let Kareen talk her into the store. She grabbed the broom as she began to get lost in her thoughts. She walked towards the door, and was startled out of thoughts by the ring of the door sounding. It slowly opened and a familiar face popped in.

"Are y'all closed?" Landon's father questioned.

# PART 16

"Well, not technically, no," Heather responded shyly. It was now the third time she had ever seen Landon's father. He looked different this time, however. It was the first time she had seen him without a beard. His clothes were clean and he didn't just barge into the door. Something was different about this time and she wondered where Landon's father had been since the incident at the hospital. Did he ever wonder about his grandkid? Did he plan on being a part of Braylen's life? She had so many questions she wanted to ask this man that she had this unfortunate connection with. She slowly walked back around the oak counter and watched while he went up and down the aisles. She didn't see him pick anything up, however, or really act interested in anything at all. He just walked slowly up and down the aisles as if he were searching for something that wasn't there. What Heather didn't know was that Frank was searching for a conversation starter. Something to bust down the door of conversation for some sort of explanation.

"I .... uh ... I like the addition of the diner." The words stuttered as they rambled out of his mouth and they almost shocked Heather.

"Yeah, we did pretty good today with it, Frank." Kareen was on the offensive. She felt she needed to protect Heather in a sense, but she was cut off. Frank didn't glance at Kareen as she gave an answer.

"Yeah," his voice trailed off and then he spoke up again. "Heather, it's been awhile. Some things have changed."

"Well, yes, Mr. Maston. We felt it needed some updating before we opened up," Heather said in a forced sweet reply.

"No, Heather, I'm talking about with me." He stared down the aisle into Heather's eyes. It was the first time she noticed that Landon and his father shared the same eyes. She got goose bumps all over as the thoughts of what he could be referring to shot off the walls of her brain. She knew with him anything was not to be unexpected. The silence in the store was only broken by the laughter of children frolicking by. Other than that, the interaction of silence between the three in the store was bone crushing.

"How is Braylen?" Frank asked, almost pleading for a welcome answer as his voice trailed off. Heather was surprised that this man was even around. How dare he have the nerve to ask about Braylen when he hadn't even been around since the day of his birth three years ago? She found herself wanting answers, so she gave in and responded.

"He's doing well. Healthy and smart. Where have you been though? You're his grandfather. I would think you would want to be in his life." She was glaring straight through him as she began to question.

"I had to disappear, Heather," Frank responded. "I know I didn't act like it, but when I lost Landon, like you, I lost everything. After your father dropped me in the hospital, I was charged with public intoxication. That night in that cold cell I sobered up and did a lot of thinking. I haven't touched alcohol since that day. I didn't come around because I knew in the state I was in I wouldn't be welcome. Besides, I didn't want my grandson, my second chance at doing something right, to see me like that. I didn't want him to know me the way my son did." His voice trailed off as a tear streamed down his face.

Heather was shocked. Here was a man that she had never seen show any type of weakness or compassion towards anything in her life and he was practically bowing down to her. She knew enough about Frank to know that this wasn't Frank. But she felt it in her heart to at least give him the chance. After all, people do change, but just in case she wouldn't let her guard down. Kareen reinforced this thought, however, before Heather could find the words for what she wanted to say.

"So what are you trying to get at with you sob story, Frank?" Kareen's voice was like a shot that broke sound barriers in Frank's direction. "You haven't been a part of the kid's life for the first three years. Why should Heather trust you and let you waltz in right now?" Kareen was quick to protect Heather and Frank was confused by the protection. Who was this woman? He had never seen her before in his life and now she wanted to act like she knew him. His anger was fuming, but he fought it down. He had a strong point to prove by coming in that store so he brushed the young female's accusations and hammered questions aside, collected his thoughts, and tried to explain.

"Just give me a chance to see him and prove a point, Heather." Once again, Frank's voice was in a pleading tone. "I missed the first three years of his life. I want to do right at least somewhere in my life." His plea had reached a point of desperation.

"Well, how should we introduce you into his life, Frank? I know you don't expect to just take off with him for the day when he doesn't even know you. A kid that age is shy and, frankly, I don't want to put him through the social shock of, 'Hey, here is your grandfather, get your coat and get the fuck out.' I can't do that to him." Heather's voice had hit the offensive tone as well. Frank knew he had done wrong by her. Hell, he had done wrong by the whole damn world, but that was done now. He refused to show any ounce of backing down from where he was coming from. That kid had two sets of grandparents and he felt that, no matter what wrong he had done, he deserved that chance. If he could just get that chance, it would make all the withdrawals, all the cold sweats, everything that came with quitting the barley and hops more than worth it. He needed a saving grace. He was pleading for a saving grace and something more to say as Heather stared coldly at him. Heather broke the repetition of excruciating silence, yet again. "I guess you could come by tomorrow after we close and follow me to my house. Better yet, I'll meet you at the coffee shop at nine-thirty tomorrow night and you can follow me home. My parents would die on the spot if I brought you to their house. It won't be long, though, as I would like to get him in bed by ten-thirty."

Frank's insides leapt with joy as he received permission. Finally, he would get a chance to find the joy behind all his sorrow. Finally, the chance to meet this kid that would be the next hometown hero and finally a chance to meet his grandson, his final connection to Landon and everything that was left right in the world for him. It was a second chance. Hell, it was more than a second chance. Frank beamed with a smile.

"Thank you for understanding, Heather. Tomorrow, nine-thirty, coffee shop. Correct? Heather nodded, her expression unchanged. "I'll be seeing you now. I really do like what you girls have done with this place. I'll have to come in more often and try that fish. I promise next time won't be this awkward," Frank finished as the door closed behind him. Heather watched Frank cross the parking lot and was startled to see him stoop down into a familiar Pinto. It was the first time she had seen Landon's car since a week before his death. That old beat up pile was looking different than three years ago, however, as it was covered in spots of body filler and primer this time instead of the familiar glossy black with rust zits. Kareen quickly yanked Heather from her thoughts about the car.

"You cannot be fucking serious about letting that old fuck waltz right in here and introduce him into your son's life. Seriously, what the fuck is wrong with you, Heather?" Kareen's voice was more than audible enough to hammer the words home for the whole town to hear.

"Kareen, I know it seems wrong, but I feel I owe it to him. You don't know Frank and I can tell he has changed. I have never seen him shaven or in clean clothes. There's not a lot that could go wrong either, it's just a short visit." Heather's voice was in a firm tone as well. She wasn't backing down from Kareen the way she always had. She firmly felt that she owed Frank the chance to see his grandson after his effort to change her thoughts. Kareen simply let out a sigh of desperation.

"I have no clue about you sometimes, Heather." Her mumbles were more than audible as she walked back behind the counter. The rest of the night was silence. No music on the ride home, no joy, only the thoughts swirling around in the heads of the two young girls. Two very different sets of thoughts they were.

# PART 17

Heather woke up the next morning wondering if she had made the right decision. After all, she didn't even know Landon's father. She just knew that he was a junkyard drunk with a scruffy beard. At any rate the beard was gone and he had showered that day. He seemed very sincere about wanting to make things right. She reassured herself as Braylen walked into her bedroom beaming his normal bright smile. Besides his hair, Braylen looked more like Landon everyday, Heather thought. Even Braylen's mumbled slang of English reminded Heather of Landon. The toddler was still everything her life was based upon. Braylen sat on the toilet and watched Heather as she straightened her hair. She burnt herself and spouted, "Dammit!" It was followed by Braylen's immediate chuckles. She couldn't help but smile herself at the sound of his sweet laughter and began to tickle him. Heather finished with her daily prep work, snatched up Braylen, and walked downstairs for breakfast.

Kareen wasn't in any better spirits today than she was the previous night. "We have half an hour untill the train leaves," Kareen said in a monotone stab.

"Ok, girl, cheer up. I know you don't agree with me letting Frank visit Braylen, but I have to try it out. Braylen has two sets of grandparents and I would like for all four to be involved instead of the usual three. You know, maybe Frank could talk Braylen into picking up a football. All he wants to do is kick that damn soccer ball around," Heather tried to lighten the subject with the sports reference. It was true, however. No matter what anyone tried, Braylen was partial to kicking things instead of throwing them.

"That man is crazy," Kareen began. "If you don't remember, I was there in the same room as you when all that drama happened. He had nothing good to say about Braylen before when he was struggling to survive and when you were laying in that hospital bed. Why should he be let in now? Heather, I know your young, but, dammit, you have to stand up for yourself whether you like it or not," Kareen finished as she sat breakfast down for the four of them.

Heather knew that Kareen was right and at some point she would have to lose that sweet innocent little girl charm. At what point would it be too much though? She agreed that she would have to harden herself a little, but she still felt solid in her reasoning on this decision. "I hope today goes as well as yesterday, Kareen. I really enjoyed it actually, you know, you and I running things the way we were. Hell, I've never even had a job; it's different." Kareen laughed as she realized how young Heather was in her country innocence. Everything in New York was more complicated than this place. Heather would never make it, Kareen thought and she began to explain.

"You have never had a job, Heather? When I was fifteen, I began working at a small bakery on the corner washing dishes. I mean, my family was middle class so we had plenty, but I didn't get anything for free. It just goes to show how much better raising kids in a small town like this is. You don't get the normal grime and sleaze of city life here." Heather simply chopped her pancakes into squares and let Kareen ramble. It was the same blah blah blah story she had heard a thousand times.

She interrupted Kareen, "Looks like we got ten minutes. I'll take the dishes to the sink," Heather got up and rinsed the fours dishes while Kareen, freshly cut off from her thoughts, gathered the kids' things.

The day began like the previous one. Heather carried the same excitement as she had embraced the day before and she was ready for everything to replay. Kareen did her normal prep of the grill area and sat down at one of the booths with a cup of coffee. Heather walked to the door, flipped the placard, and sat down across from Kareen in the booth. The two sat and sipped on their steamy beverages for a few minutes before Kareen finally spoke up.

"Heather, I'm sorry for the way I acted. It's just I feel something bad about this whole situation of you letting Frank in that easy. Just be safe about it, girl. I would hate to have to go crazy on someone because you or Braylen got hurt." Heather was surprised at Kareen's apology as Kareen had never backed down from anything she said in the time Heather had known her.

"It means a lot that you understand my side of everything in this as well, Kareen. And don't you worry, there is no way in hell that I am going to allow him to be alone with Braylen or keep him alone for some time. He has to prove things with me, Kareen. I'm not just letting him in. I'm not that crazy." With the last sentence, Kareen laughed and Heather was thrown off her thoughts.

"You *are* that crazy," Kareen joked. Heather blushed and sipped some more coffee as the door chime rang its usual annoying chime for the first time that day. "Well, let's get to work," Kareen said and the two walked to opposite ends of the store.

\* \* \*

The day flew by for Heather and she was glad because as the day grew longer, she grew more anxious for the interaction between Braylen and his grandfather. The store closed at nine, but Heather had all her cleaning done by eight-thirty because she was so ready to get out the door and just get this first visit over with.

"Heather, get out of here or you're going to be late," Kareen scolded at nine-oh-five.

"Ok, girl. I will see you back at the house at about ten. I'm just going to grab Braylen from my parent's and have coffee and get home. I don't plan on staying out too late. Why don't you stay up so we can talk about it when I get home and have a glass of wine?" Heather questioned as she was fumbling for her keys and heading for the door. "I'm getting kind of nervous about this one now. Do you think I should do it?" Heather questioned Kareen sincerely.

"Well, it's a little late now, girl," Kareen answered with a smile. "See you at ten." Heather walked briskly to her car and headed towards the adventure.

Frank was already at the coffee shop sitting in the little Pinto waiting for Heather. Braylen was in a cheerful mood and Heather was thankful for this. If he was in one of his crabby moods, this meeting would not be up to par. Frank stepped out of the tiny car when Heather pulled up and opened her door for her with a beaming smile. Heather could read the excitement on the man's still clean shaven face. He had actually had another set of fresh clothes on as well. "Glad you didn't stand me up, kiddo," he said jokingly as Heather started to unbuckle Braylen from his booster seat.

"Well, I was nervous, but I figured I owed you the chance, even if it was over coffee," Heather said in an honest response.

"Do you come here often?" Frank asked, trying to create conversation as they ambled side by side through the parking lot to the door. Braylen was skipping and babbling about the birds being up so late. Braylen believed everything should be inside at dark time because it was mom's rule. Heather remembered that cute conversation like it was yesterday. Frank held the door for Heather and Braylen and then the three walked inside.

Heather ordered mocha for herself and a cup of chocolate milk for Braylen. The little shop was already halfway done with her order by the time she had finished. It was her normal everyday order they had grown used to. She then went to grab for her money and Frank cut her off.

"Add a large black to that please," Frank asked the teenager as he grabbed for his wallet. "You're nice enough to meet me here after your long day. I have this one covered," Frank said with a smile in Heather's direction. Heather could tell he was sincere, but she was even more shocked to see that his fingernails were groomed as well as his shave. It was something her grandfather had told her jokingly when she started dating Landon. "You can tell a lot by a man by his fingernails and if they are clean," Heather could hear her grandpa's raspy voice in the back of her head. Frank was thoroughly clean now, it seemed, and he smelled lightly of aftershave instead of the normal Jack and Coke. The three walked, Braylen skipping, to the closet booth and then sat down. Heather began to introduce Braylen to his grandfather, but the toddler cut her off.

"Grandpa!" Braylen spouted with a bubbly smile. Frank's face lit up as well. How in the hell did he know who Frank is? Heather's brain went spastic as it began to process the turn.

# PART 18

It was if Braylen had already met Frank before and Heather's brain couldn't process it. Frank saw Heather struggling with what had just happened. He knew she didn't know about the visits that had already been taking place over the last month. While Heather was at the store working to get things in place, Frank was visiting Braylen at her parents' house. He had tracked down her number in an attempt to track down his grandson, not knowing she moved out of the house. Her parents were not nearly as accepting as Heather had been and Dan emitted the same warning. But after a stop by at Heather's house, her parents gave in. It was their idea that Frank come and visit Heather at the store because Heather's parents didn't feel right about all the secrecy and, well, Frank couldn't help but agree. How was he to explain to Heather that he had been seeing her child behind her back? It was suddenly more difficult than he had pictured it, but he knew something had to be said.

"Looking for an explanation?" Frank offered in Heather's direction. She was shocked that he noticed how stunned she had been and almost couldn't say yes. How could this stranger have the explanation for what had just happened? Frank didn't know Braylen from the next kid or so she thought. Heather was clueless in the matter and could not find it. "Heather, this is not the first time I have seen Braylen," Frank started. "While you were working at the store getting everything ready to open, I stopped by your parent's house and they let me see him . . . . But I know what you're thinking, they didn't just let me in that easy. Hell, they gave me more of a fight than you, but after all, I am working here and he is my grandson." Heather was fuming and she cut him off.

"Yeah, well, he's my fucking son! How dare you guys just go behind my back like that?" She couldn't believe that her parents would go behind her back for this stranger. Her mother was the most protective and her father had dropped this man three years prior. How was it in their right to show off her kid?

"Heather calm down. You're scaring Braylen," Frank said, pleading for some sort of let up. Heather was caught off guard and looked over at Braylen. The toddler was, in fact, staring up at her as if she were an alien from some distant planet. She knew she shouldn't be speaking like that in front of him while he was in such a impressionable stage in his life. She began again, softer this time, and without the angst.

"Frank, when did you and my parents figure this was a good idea and why didn't you check with me first?"

"Well," he started, "it wasn't as easy as it sounds. I tracked down your phone number, Heather, because I figured you probably still lived at home. Well, I called one day and found out otherwise. The first time when your mother answered the phone, she instantly hung up." Heather's eyes were glaring across at Frank as he spoke, but he continued, "Your mom eventually told me a little about what had been going on with you; about how you moved out to the house with Kareen." He paused and with a smile said, "Man, she's a spitfire," with a chuckle.

"Well, before we get to all that, tell me what should make me believe you have changed, Frank," Heather challenged him.

"Well, like I told you in the store, Heather, after your dad took that swing and I ended up in the clink that night, a lot hit me. It never really weighed on me that Landon was really gone until all this happened. That boy was my world, and I regret almost every second of parenthood and how I raised him. I woke up the next morning in cold sweats craving a beer, but knew I had to do better for my grandson." Heather's expression was growing softer as she listened to the man speak. He continued in earnest, "I just knew I had to do right this time, so I did the only thing I knew how to do besides drink. I stayed at my junkyard. I stayed there and cleaned the place up, did the simple things like mow, fix the fence, just make the place presentable so a business could actually be ran out of there. I have been fixing cars up as well and selling them for cheap. You know since the settlement with the coal plant, when Landon was a baby, I don't have to worry about money, but I had to get through the alcohol. I had to get past it. I knew there was a thing in this life that I hadn't experienced yet and that I probably never would if I didn't leave that bottle behind"

Heather's mind was racing to try to find a way to believe she should trust this man. She wanted to and she had to. It was just all so hard. She wished that her parents would have let her handle this like an adult. She wondered how that came about, so she asked, "Why did it take so long for you to feel like you needed to tell me?"

He had obviously prepared to be grilled with that question and so began, "It was your mom's idea. She wanted to protect you against me, I figure. She didn't want you out on your own with that child with a man that she didn't trust. Even though you're not home you're still your mother's baby girl, Heather, and I'm sure you always will be. You have to accept that your parents will always try to take up for you whether you want them to or not." Heather was tired of the lecture so she cut him off.

"Ok, I get it, just where do we go from here? How much does he really know you? I mean, what type of time have you spent with my son behind my back?" Heather found herself questioning everything. She wanted answers and she wanted them fast; faster than Frank was giving them. She stayed calm, however, for Braylen's sake and let the man begin another explanation.

"I would say it's been about a total of eight hours. It's been enough for him to know who I am and call me by that title, as you can see." Frank shot Braylen a quick smile and could tell the toddler was growing impatient with the lack of attention. Frank reached over and grabbed Braylen and started bouncing him on his knee. As he looked up and across the table, he could see the obvious glare of disgust in her face, but continued anyways. "The first day it was probably half an hour, but it was the same format we are following here. Your mother grilled me for hours on end about everything; where I had been, my past . . . that woman didn't let up." Heather smiled as she heard Frank describe her mother. She knew he probably went through hell getting through Lisa to Braylen. She was glad for every second of it. She continued to listen to Frank's explanation. "Well, the second day, it was probably an hour. They invited me over to supper and let me play with him. It made me feel like a kid again playing around in the yard tossing a ball back and forth. We may have to get his brain looked at, though. He likes to kick more than throw." They both chuckled at the small joke because the whole town was relying on that kid to grow into some sort of football star. Heather was satisfied so she cut him off.

"Well, Frank, I don't like it but it's already over. We will just have to go from here, but I have to be getting home. It's getting late."

Frank led the two out to the car and attempted an awkward hug, gave Braylen a kiss on the forehead, and both groups parted ways. Heather spent the whole drive home questioning everything the man had told her. It was all obviously true what he was saying, but she couldn't wrap her head around the idea that her mother had just let him in. I mean, Frank said that her mother had given him a fight, but she wasn't comfortable with the fact that her mother felt she could just make those types of decisions for Braylen without even including Heather. She also knew that it was probably pointless to dwell on it because there wasn't a thing she could do about it at the time. The damage was already there and at least she wasn't the one having to explain to Braylen who Frank was. It was all just madness and she got tired of thinking about it so she attempted a few duets with the toddler, but soon realized he was fast asleep in the back seat. She wished he would stay that size forever. Just old enough that those diapers were no longer needed, but young enough to be invincible to the problems of the world.

"Please stay that size forever," she whispered back to him as she turned in the drive.

# PART 19

She walked into the house and Kareen was on the couch sipping some of the familiar Sunday night wine. She could tell that Heather was upset, but she decided not to pry. She watched Heather as she walked up the stairs and down the fall to the kids' room. Kareen still couldn't get over Heather's beauty and she wanted more than anything to follow her up to that room and push her into her own. She knew it wasn't the right answer, though. They had talked it over before, and there hadn't been any incidents in the last couple years. Kareen was ok with her feelings, but Heather was not. Kareen still had the same plans, however, to keep Heather around and make her fall for what she was scared of. Whatever it could be, Kareen believed that she could change it. She pushed aside her thoughts, however, to try and figure out what was bothering Heather.

"What's wrong, Heather?" Kareen called to her as she was walking down the steps with the troubled look still on her face.

"Well, the craziest thing took place today, hun. First, let me get a glass of what you're having, though. I so need it," Heather answered as she walked past the living room into the kitchen. She grabbed a wine glass out of the cupboard. They were a light blue, Kareen's favorite color. She then grabbed a bottle of wine and then poured herself a glass, and this time, as full as she could get it. She knew tonight was going to need some stress relief, so she took a sip and then grabbed the bottle and carried both to the living room. She let herself sink into the dark blue couch beside Kareen and caught the woman's concerned glance. She took a few sips and then asked, "What are we going to watch tonight Kar?"

Kareen brushed away the question and followed up, "The movie doesn't matter, Love. What matters is that vein sticking out on your neck. Tell me how everything went."

"Well," Heather began as she took a gulp from the bottle, completely forgetting about the glass. "Apparently, my parents were letting Frank see Braylen behind my back. My mother sent him to the store that day to try to get me to be ok with it. I really don't understand what the fuck she was thinking by doing that. I mean, he is my kid, after all. What right does she have?" Kareen didn't feel like that was really a question she should answer so she left it open ended. She thought it was cute when Heather was upset, but she was still concerned. Heather had stopped talking and took another swig of the bottle. She had already consumed more than the nightly glass and her glass was still full.

"Give me that," Kareen said. "Now continue your story." Heather gave up the bottle reluctantly and paused long enough to watch Kareen take a drink. She was surprised that she was already feeling the effects from the first few swigs. She continued, the words flowing a little freer this time.

"Like I was saying, my parents let Frank see Braylen behind my back. He started coming over while we were working on the store. Imagine that. They think they know what is best for Braylen and figured it would be best to just go around my back with this shit." Heather was growing irate at this time. Kareen had only seen this side of her a few times before. Heather grabbed the bottle took a swig and set it on the coffee table. She started to begin again, "They . . . ." She was cut off. Kareen had seen too much and held back for two long. She reached over and put one hand on Heather's cheek while she slowly kissed the girl. Heather didn't put up a fight, she merely kissed back. Her head wasn't swarming like it had been before. She didn't know if it was the alcohol, or what it was, but she was comfortable in this kiss. Kareen pushed her back onto the couch, gave her a long passionate deep kiss, and then paused to stare her in the eyes.

"It will all be okay, babe," Kareen whispered. "You have your family here and you have me," she further explained, never letting her eyes unlock from Heather's. Those blue eyes burned into the back of her head and she went for a second kiss. This one, too, was accepted and Heather brought her hand to rest on the small of Kareen's back, used her other hand to pull a blanket down across them, and then switched on the movie. It had been awhile since she cuddled with anyone. She missed that feeling.

The couple lay on the couch and watched the movie. Heather found herself running her hands through Kareen's hair while the girl rested her head on Heather's chest. The only thing shocking about this incident to Heather was that she felt so comfortable with it. Everything about that kiss seemed right and she felt her lips begging to taste more. She held herself back, though, and tried to concentrate on watching the movie. She didn't wish for things to go farther because she didn't want to hit the awkward stage. She knew there were things that they could do further, but she also wanted to just let the kisses linger for as long as possible. It had been a long time since she had been touched in a sexual manner, and she longed for it, but wondered if it would freak her out. She knew she was comfortable with the kisses, but couldn't lock her thoughts on what she would do if anything went farther. She kissed Kareen on the forehead and the girl smiled up at her. She remembered how comfortable that had made her feel when Landon had done it and she could sense the same comfort in Kareen's body language now.

"How about you sleep with me tonight?" Kareen almost pleaded. "We will talk to your parents tomorrow."

* * *

The rest of the night went like the beginning. The two girls walked sleepily up to the bedroom. Heather stripped down to a t shirt and underwear and Kareen did the same. Kareen then playfully pushed Heather back on the bed and crawled up to her, ending with a sweet soft kiss, but nothing further happened. They fell asleep in each other's arms and Heather woke up feeling refreshed. It was the first time she had slept that comfortably in a long time and she let her mind wander to what she thought the relationship should be. She wondered if she would begin sleeping with Kareen every night. She not only wondered, but welcomed the idea. Kareen still carried that presence that everything was going to be alright and Heather loved it. She felt energized like a kid again and it was hard for her not to move and wake Kareen. She gave into the urges, however, and slid herself out from underneath Kareen's grasp. She put on a bra and a pair of shorts, and watched Kareen sleep for a moment. She looked so peaceful to Heather. Heather leaned down, gave her a kiss, and walked downstairs. She felt she could manage to cook breakfast today and surprise Kareen.

Kareen was thoroughly surprised to wake up to the aroma of breakfast. When she walked downstairs, Braylen and Steph were in the living room watching the normal Monday morning cartoons. The girls had asked Heather's parents to run the store today, which they instantaneously agreed to. Kareen had the intentions, however, of stopping by that day to see how things were going and they had to make a visit at Heather's parents that night to sort out the Frank issues. Kareen brushed it out of her head though, finished spying on the children, and then made the trek to the kitchen. Heather was in there working feverishly on something that looked pathetically like pancakes. Kareen walked over and smiled at Heather, gave her a quick kiss, and questioned, "So, um, breakfast, Heather?"

"Well, it's an attempt at breakfast," Heather responded with a nervous laugh.

"I have to teach you how to cook, don't I?" Kareen offered.

"Sure, babe. Teach me all you know." Heather had called Kareen babe and it struck that butterfly releasing nerve in Kareen. Finally, things were turning.

# PART 20

The two drove to the store the next day at about two-thirty. Heather's parents were inside and things seemed to be going well. As always, the diner was full and the elderly couples were discussing the normal gossip around the town. Apparently, the town had another star quarterback this year.

"He won't be near as good in the fourth quarter as Landon. He was unbreakable under pressure." Heather heard one of the old men discussing the upcoming season. She was surprised. It had been this long and everyone still remembered Landon enough to call him by his first name. She wondered when that would die out. When does a hero become just a memory? A few words on an old Sunday newspaper was all she knew that he would ever amount to now. He would be just a distant memory in a town that hung onto the young people as if they were the life of everything. That small high school was the life of everything in that town and it was shown everyday as Heather overheard the elderly talking about the upcoming sports who's who. They all grew quiet with the sports talk as they watched Heather walking down the aisle. They always changed the subject in respect for her on this matter.

"How are things looking, Lisa?" Kareen called from behind Heather. "You able to keep up alright?" Lisa looked up with a bright smile.

"Girls, this is the most I've done in years. You really do need to thank your father, Heather, for coming in here on his day off. I swear though, he's having more fun in here than he would at home lounging on the couch. He's talked everyone's ear off that's gone past that old cash register. We will do this for you anytime you girls wish." Heather did not pay attention to her mother's warm welcome and gave a quick snotty response.

"I guess I can trust you more here than I can with Braylen, huh, mother?" The elderly suddenly grew quiet at the exchange of words that just tickled their ears.

"Do you have something we need to talk about honey?" Lisa answered in a bewildered response.

"Yes. Yes, I do, mother, but not here. We will talk somewhere else where it won't end up the talk of the town." Lisa simply stared at her, stunned at her daughter's attitude.

Dan had caught the interaction between the two females between his exchanges at the counter. He knew the two women in his life and couldn't hear what they were saying, but could tell by body language that some trouble was brewing.

"Heather," he called, "will you come up here to show me how to work something?" Dan had really no questions at all, he had just wanted to pull Heather and Lisa apart. The two of them were arguing so much now days and they would never tell him what it was all about. Heather did as he asked and made her way to the front of the store, the expression on her face never changing. She stopped for a moment to swoop up Braylen in her arms as he was trying to play with something on a shelf and continued towards her father. "What's wrong, honey?" Dan said in a whisper as his daughter rounded the counter.

"Well, father, I got to talk with Frank yesterday. It would have been nice to know you guys were parading my kid around without asking me first. How did you perceive this to be a good idea?" Dan was shocked as Heather sent the searing question in his direction. Heather had never used that tone with him before. He searched for words to explain. Dan knew that Heather had every reason to be upset and he began to try to explain in a confused tone.

"Baby, you know Braylen had to know his grandfather sometime or another. Frank has really gotten cleaned up and we, me and your mother, felt it was ok to let Frank visit." Heather cut him off as she no longer wanted to hear any further explanation.

"I know the story, father. I just wanted to try to understand what made you guys think it was such a damn good idea to do behind my back. Braylen is my child, you know. I should be the one making all the decisions, not you two. How can I trust you guys watching my kid everyday if you won't even tell me what you're doing with him?" Dan didn't answer the question in any type of depth. He knew that Heather was right, but also felt offended that she didn't trust Lisa and him with Braylen. They would never do anything to hurt the child.

Heather stormed out of the store with Braylen in tow. She walked to the car, got in, and waited on Kareen to join. Kareen came out a few short minutes later and turned towards the car with a beaming grin on her face.

"Well, crazy, you're sure to be the talk of this small town now," Kareen shot at Heather as she climbed in the passenger seat. "You think you could have waited 'till you were alone with them tonight? You know we have to come back and collect the deposit box," Kareen explained. "I was hoping you would wait till then."

"I was planning on it," Heather began, "but I get so tired of people thinking they can do whatever the hell they want and it just be ok with me. When I walked inside the store and saw my mother so cheerful, it just set me off. She knows what she did and I plan on making her well aware that it pisses me off. Like I told them, Braylen is my child and I have the final say over what he does or who is in his life," Heather continued to rant as she drove.

"You know, it's not so bad, Heather," Kareen offered some sympathy to Lisa and Dan. "You know as well as I do that if Frank had seen Braylen you would have given him no chance that night when you met with him. I could see it on your face that you were only doing it because you felt you owed him the chance. Your mind was made up when you walked out that door that things were not going to go well and I could see that. Personally, I think it's wrong that they went behind your back and did something like that, but at the same time, hell, at least it's out of the way. Everybody you could possibly want in your son's life for his welfare sake is there. They have even adopted Steph as one of their own since her grandparents and family are so far away. Give 'em some slack, baby. It's not so bad." Heather could feel the rage inside her subsiding with Kareen's explanation. Once again, Kareen had cooled her fire, but she wasn't going to let Kareen know, so she gave no response as she continued towards the park where they had set a play date for the kids. Heather cranked the music up and the two began to sing their normal duet.

Once they were at the park they sat at a bench and began to talk as the kids played on the various obstacles. "Kareen, I know your right. I just. . . . I guess I'm just protective over Braylen. He is the only thing I have left of Landon and even though it's been over three years now, I still miss him. I never knew how deep a mother's love really is until I had the little bundle. The whole time I was pregnant I hated it and the consequences it held, but you know what? Now that I'm here, I wouldn't take any of it back," Heather began to explain as everything inside her just felt tangled at the day's events.

"Heather, I know exactly what you're talking about. I feel the exact same way with Steph and with Jason's kids. I miss them every day now, but it's life and, just like you, I wouldn't take a single footstep back. We make an amazing pair raising these kids on our own. Just look where we are at. Single mothers supporting ourselves and doing a damn good job at it, if I must say so myself," Kareen began to give explanations of her own. Heather scooted closer to Kareen and laid her head on the woman's shoulder. She knew that Kareen must be feeling the same exact thing as she was. She felt like nothing could ever go wrong, it was a feeling she had started to carry a lot and she liked it because she was growing tired of the uncertainty before. She would apologize to her parents that night, but only for the sake of Braylen, and she would let them know in a little softer tone that they were still wrong. That could wait, however. She just wanted to focus on right now.

# PART 21

Kareen sensed Heather's generally decent mood and it warmed her inside as well. She loved that she still had that affect on the younger girl and she knew it was partially what kept Heather around. She did feel protective over Heather in a motherly sense and she felt that she probably always would. The two of them sat on the bench and watched the children as they ran around the well kept playground. Kareen shared in the same feelings of just wanting to sit there for awhile and take everything in. She finally had Heather right where she wanted her and life was all good. She was going to ride the rollercoaster for as long as the park was open. Heather was addicting and every kiss left Kareen craving more of Heather, but she knew it was too early and she didn't want to scare her young love away from the new found rendezvous they were on. In all due time, though, she would unleash the seductive powers she had used before, but never on a female. The two of them sat silently, never knowing they shared almost identical thoughts about the relationship. Each only knew the simple fact that they were happy.

"Mommy, will you push us?" Braylen called out as he ran with his little legs in her direction. Both the girls stood up and walked over to the swings. Heather was pushing Steph, and Kareen, Braylen. It was their own little family. Steph and Braylen had bonded in a way that was different from a family bond. It was almost like they knew they weren't related in any way, but had that bond that a brother and sister share. The children had taken special interest in different sports and such, which was not unusual for such a young age in a small town. When the summer came, each child had plans of playing on the community soccer team. The teams were created to train the young boys how to track the ball in preparation for their venture into football. Braylen took a different step with the sport however, and even though he was little, he seemed to strive for competition. Everything he did, he had to do better. Whether it was swinging higher or helping around the house, there were no limits to what he would turn into a game.

Heather knew he had to carry this mentality if he was ever to grow up to be what that town needed him for. It was such a young age, but she knew that, so far, the child had shown no interest in football. She knew she would stand behind him, whatever he chose.

"Do you think it's a good idea to let them play soccer this summer, Kar?" Heather questioned trying to determine her partner's thoughts on what was already running in her head.

"Well, it couldn't hurt, Heather. I mean, it's just a bunch of kids running around kicking at a ball. It would be good for their health to be involved with something like that and it will give us some time apart from the daily grind of being a mother." It was another brilliant explanation, Heather thought to herself. Kareen had found more things good about the situation than what Heather had even touched. Heather looked at it from the angle of what the town would feel about what the kids were doing and Kareen was focusing on what was good for the family and the health of the children. It was a mentality that Heather wished she could pick up. She hated that she still cared what everyone in that small town said about her and her child. She always denied it, but she cared.

"So, what's troubling you with it?" Kareen questioned Heather, as she could tell she was deep in thought. The veins across Heather's temple always seemed to stick out just a little more when Heather was deep in thought. It was another one of the faces Kareen learned to pick up on fast.

"Well, you just . . . you explain things so well, Kareen and I just wish I could be like you more as a mother." Heather was just as shocked as Kareen at the praise she had just given.

"Thanks, babe, but don't kid yourself. You're a damn good mother for your son. Look how far you have come without his father and at such a young age," Kareen returned the praise.

"I know I'm a good mom, Kareen. It's just that we approach things different and I feel I'm a little more selfish than I should be. When I asked you about the kids it wasn't because of what I felt, it's because I know the town wants Braylen to grow up to be the next football king of the universe or something. I just wish that I could forget about what everyone else thought and just raise my child," Heather finished the confession and it all really shocked Kareen to hear Heather admit these things. She pushed Braylen for a few more swings and tried to address Heather to somehow make the girl feel better about the situation.

"Like I said before, Heather," Kareen began, "you're a damn good mother. You're just young and you're used to the high school life still. Hell, it was two weeks ago for you." She paused to let the joke sit on Heather and saw a smile slowly creep on her face. She then continued,

"You just have to learn to accept that as a mother you're not going to do everything right, Heather. You have to know that everything you do, as long as you do it in love, is in the best interest of your child and there's nothing wrong with mistakes. Be easier on yourself, babe," Kareen finished the explanation and from the looks of Heather's expression, the motherly tactic had worked yet again. The sun was starting to go down once again on the sleepy town and the mothers let gravity do the work on slowing the children to a stop. Heather felt a hand go around her waist as they were watching the children and Kareen snuggled up to her side. Heather didn't question it; she just stood there waiting for the children to stop. Once they stopped, the girls rounded the children up and began to head to the car.

Once in the car, they all drove to the little ice cream shop in the town and all enjoyed an ice cream cone. Of course, in his new competitive edge, Braylen made sure to finish his ice cream cone first and then skipped around the table waiting for the other three to finish. Kareen looked at Heather and with her usually spontaneous way asked, "What do you think about Frank coaching a soccer team?" The question took Heather by surprise, but only because of the randomness at which it had arrived. She had come to expect these things from Kareen. She milled it over in her head for a second as she finished more of the ice cream.

"Well, what do you think of it first?" Heather countered Kareen's question with another question. If she knew one thing, she knew that Kareen wouldn't ask any questions without already having an answer lined up. Kareen acted as if she was thinking about her answer, but in fact, Heather was correct and she had one lined up already.

"Well, babe, I think it's a pretty solid idea. I mean, Frank wants to be involved in Braylen's life as much as you will let him and that's a way to do it without really letting him be alone. At the same time, you will be including him in a significant amount of time each day in Braylen's life. I think it will work out just fine and, hell, it will get that old man out of that damn junk yard." Heather nodded in approval and Kareen went on to explain, "I know nothing about this man. Only the times I've been able to act like a complete smart ass in his direction." Heather laughed as Kareen brought back memories of the day in the store when the girl had grilled Frank.

"Yeah, you really lit him up there, didn't ya, girl?" They both smiled for a second and Kareen began to map out her plans to Heather. "How about you get a hold of him tonight after we get back and invite him over for dinner tomorrow? Signups for coaching is in two weeks and players three weeks. If we can get him backed into it, it will work." Heather nodded in approval and they began walking back to the car.

"Let's go get our money," Heather said with a smile.

## PART 22

The short drive to the store was uneventful. It was a beautiful night with a full moon that lit up the country town nicely. You could sense the oncoming of summer from the high school kids out running around trying to get in shape for the upcoming sports' seasons. As all small towns, this one strived off of sports. It was part of everyone's way of life. Even at three years old, Braylen and Steph were already living the effect of sports. Heather was thinking to herself how she was going to get Frank talked into coaching the little league soccer team. She knew he loved sports, and mostly football, but soccer was considered a disease in that small town. She wondered if Frank would try to talk them out of letting Braylen play the "fairy sport" or if he would embrace it altogether and just run with it. She was wishing for the latter, and knew that Kareen would probably have him like a scared dog with his tail tucked and running by the end of dinner the next day. The thoughts created a smile on her face as they pulled into the girls' place of business.

Once out of their booster seats, Braylen and Steph ran inside to tell the grandparents the news. Apparently, they were too quick for Heather because she walked in the door and her father was already questioning.

"So soccer, huh, babe . . . ." He smiled in her direction. He knew what it would mean to the small town that this kid wasn't aiming to be some football god as his daddy had been. He didn't let on to Heather, however, and began to prod trying to get a response. "What will the town think when little Braylen here is not donning that silver and black uniform for that school in twelve years babe" She looked at him and, knowing her dad, just brushed the comment off.

"I don't really care what they think as long as my boy is happy, pops," she said with a smile. He was put off that she wasn't jumping up to her guard so he could harass her some more, but he was proud of his daughter for putting her son above what that town wanted. He knew there would be flack from every direction, but he was like Heather and didn't care as long as his grandkid, well, grandkids including Steph, were happy. The toddler, still excited from the news, grabbed a couple lollipops from the counter dish and sat in a booth giggling and bubbling with the overbearing excitement.

"Well, how well did we do today guys?" Kareen asked with an inviting smile.

"Well, besides a girl walking in here and getting nuts on me, everything went without issues," Lisa replied with a poke at Heather.

"Yeah, about that, mom, I'm sorry. Just next time, you know, I need to be kept in the loop on those type of things. You guys may have done me a favor actually in the long run." Lisa was surprised that the new version of her daughter was apologizing, but she welcomed it. She knew that Heather had definitely turned into her own person and an adult in the few short years Braylen had been around. She knew also that she was in the wrong for letting Frank visit without Heather's permission. She knew her daughter, so her attention was drawn to the "favor in the long run" portion of the conversation.

"What do you mean 'favor in the long run,' babe?" Lisa questioned.

"Well, we were at the park, mom, and Kareen had one of her brilliant ideas," Heather began a bubbly explanation. She always used an upbeat tone when she felt she really had a good worthwhile idea. "We're calling Frank tonight and since he wants to be part of Braylen's life, we are going to give him a pretty big position," Heather paused and looked over at Kareen as she was knelt down beside the kids tickling and poking around with them. She truly was an amazing mother.

"Well, go on," Lisa pried growing anxious with the pause in the conversation.

"Yeah, well, we are going to call him tonight and see if he wants to come out and eat tomorrow. You know, make it sound innocent, but in turn we have a way of saving that old man. After we get his belly full, Kareen is going to throw the idea of coaching a soccer team for the children. Hell, it would allow him a chance to really get to know Braylen and be a huge part of his life, but at the same time it will be indirectly supervised from all the parents at practice. Also, for the old man's sake, it will get him away from that dreaded junk hole."

Lisa thoroughly thought it was an amazing scheme of getting Frank wrapped up in Braylen's life without really giving him too much room to roam. It would also give the girls some free time since all they did was work at the grocery store and then go straight home.

"So, what are you guys going to fix?" Lisa showed her approval as she asked the question.

"Well . . . uh . . . we are . . ." Heather began to respond, but was cut off.

"*We* are not cooking anything. Shame on you, Lisa. Heather here is horrible in the kitchen." Kareen let the joke sink in and it was obvious Dan had caught it because out of the corner of Kareen's eye she could see the man doubled over trying not to laugh as he stared out the storefront window. "I think *I'm* just going to cook pepper steak and the normal sides. Ya know, with a man, you can never go wrong with steak." Kareen finished with a smile in Lisa's direction. Lisa was glad the hostility from earlier that day had gone and inside she admired Kareen for what she had done. Heather had come a long way since she moved into that, at the time, random girl's house. Lisa hated the attitude Heather had picked up from Kareen, but she could not argue on the overall package.

Dan decided to fire a question in the girl's direction. "I know it's only been a couple days since you guys have opened, but you're obviously going to make a nice profit. Have you guys thought of maybe hiring some help for the summer so that you guys can have some free time? Hell, you could pay four or five high school kids minimum wage pretty easy, probably, with a store this size. Then you guys could have a lot more free time. The one thing you don't want to do is miss your kids growing up because you were stuck at this store. I know it's early, but it's just something to think about," Dan finished the idea, and waited for a response. He knew with Kareen and his daughter that Kareen would probably take the lead.

"That really seems like a good idea," Kareen said after a few moments. "Will you draft up some applications for us, Dan? I'm not very good with that sort of thing at all." Heather agreed with the idea as well and they all began to clean up the little store.

While they were cleaning, Heather got lost in her normal thoughtful state. She wondered how Kareen was able to make decisions that fast. The idea hadn't even registered in her mind before Kareen shot Dan the answer, but Heather knew it was the right answer. Her dad was right, and with all the hours she was spending at the small store, she was missing out on a small part of her child's life. She figured that even though it would reduce profits a little, that it would be better in the long run. She wondered who she trusted, though, with the store and which of the high schoolers in that country town would take something like that serious. She tried to brush the ideas out of her head, though, and realized that she was taking it way too seriously. She looked up from sweeping and watched Braylen and Steph for a few moments. He was still the best thing that had happened to her in her life and she couldn't believe how much he changed her future. She wouldn't take a second back though.

"Well, it looks like we are pretty done here," Lisa said to no one in particular and withdrew Heather from her thoughts. "We will get out of you girls' hair now. I know I could use a hot bath and you guys need to get those children to bed. The money's on the counter in the deposit bag," Lisa finished her explanation with a smile and began to head for the door with Dan trailing. Once at the door, Lisa walked out, but Dan paused for a moment and looked back at the girls.

"Do you think Frank could use an assistant coach?" he said in an almost childish tone.

"He sure will," Heather said with a smile.

# PART 23

The following day, Heather called Frank early in the morning. "So, would you like to come for dinner?" Heather questioned into the phone, refusing to even hint that there would be any further motives except for good food and company.

"Why, sure," Frank answered jubilantly through his end of the call. "How about seven? I know it's late, but I have some work I have to get done before I close up for the day. Business is taking off, ya know?" He tried not to let Heather catch on to how excited he truly was. He simply embraced the fact that some normalcy had come back into his life. Heather could sense it, however, and she knew that Kareen would tear him apart once she got the man's stomach full. She was like a piranha when she smelled blood and she had a keen sense for when people were the most vulnerable. She would wait for him to be the most vulnerable and sneak it up on him. Heather chuckled as she pictured it in her head.

"Well, the bait has been set and I think the fish are going to bite today," Heather called into Kareen. Heather then walked into the dining room to see Kareen and the children laughing. Breakfast was already in front of them all.

"What kind of country gibberish is that, babe?" Kareen stumbled across the words as she laughed. Heather felt her face growing red with embarrassment.

"Well, it makes perfect sense to me," she jumped to her own defense, trying not to pout. She dug into her pancakes as the laughter died down.

"Well, do you think he will bite on it?" Kareen questioned as she sipped on some orange juice.

"Are you kidding me?" Heather said in a surprised tone. "Girl, have you ever not got your way? I mean, look at me, I'm at your house sleeping in your bed, working at our store. None of those were my ideas."

"Yeah, but you're a little pushover," Kareen cut her off with a big smile. Heather laughed this time instead of showing embarrassment, grabbed her and the children's plate, and began to take it into the kitchen.

"Well, what about mine?" Kareen questioned with a pout.

"That's what you get for making fun at me already this morning," Heather retaliated with her near perfect smile. They grabbed their things and began to head to the store. They dropped the kids of at Heather's parent's house along the way.

"Do you think he will bite?" Lisa questioned as she received the children.

"Well, mom, as well as we know Kareen, do you think he even has a chance?" Heather returned the question. Lisa began to laugh because she knew exactly what her daughter was saying. The rest of the drive to the store was accompanied by the normal singing and when they made it to the store they began to go through the normal motions and opened right on time. The clock was ticking ever so slowly in Heather's opinion she just wanted it to hit three o'clock because that's when her parents were taking over. She wanted to just get this day over with so that she knew for sure what direction things would be going in. She knew that Frank stood no chance against a willful Kareen, but there was always that doubt nagging at the back of her head. The time slowly crept and, finally, it was three. The girls changed over duties at the store and drove to their home with children in tow.

Once at the house both went upstairs to dress down into some cleaning and cooking clothes. Both wore a white tank top with short shorts. Heather's beauty stuck Kareen when she turned around and they went to walk out the door. Kareen stepped in front of Heather with a beaming smile and said in an excited tone, "Where do you think you're going, punk?"

Heather knew the look in her eyes and her face lit up as well. She squeezed Kareen at the most ticklish points on her waist and Kareen pushed her back to the bed. Both were engulfed in laughter as they wrestled about. Kareen eventually got Heather to her back and straddled her legs around the girl's waist, holding down her arms with her own. Heather submitted to the obviously stronger Kareen and began to use the one power she knew she had over her mate. She began to stare directly into Kareen's eyes. It had the exact effect she was aiming for and she almost instantaneously felt herself being pushed back into the white comforter with a forceful kiss. She felt a soft touch begin to run up her thigh and felt a sense of doubt wash over her. She played it off, however, and whispered up at the girl, "No fun time for you. We got dinner to make, momma." Kareen was put off and she gave Heather one last deep kiss before standing up and helping Heather up off the bed. Both went downstairs to begin the chores.

* * *

Frank arrived a little later than the prescribed time, but it was actually a good thing for the girls. Somehow in their incident, they had lost track of time and were running a little late themselves. Heather walked out onto the wraparound porch as Frank got out of a newer truck that had replaced the Pinto. "Where's the old Pinto?" Heather questioned.

"Well I'm actually restoring it back to factory with a couple tweaks, well major tweaks, of my own. It gives me a certain connection I feel to you-know-who. I bought this trying to treat myself to the finer things in life. You know, dropping alcohol frees up a lot of money." Heather smiled, satisfied by Frank's explanation and opened the gate for the man to step into the yard. "This place is beautiful, Heather. I have never seen it before in all my years of living in this small community. And this yard, who are you having keep this up for you?" Frank was thoroughly impressed.

"Well, Kareen takes care of it. I don't know what we will do now that we got the store open." Frank was further impressed and admired its beauty a few seconds further as he walked through the front door of the house.

The dinner conversation was kept light with intermittent laughter due to the toddler's shenanigans here and there. Frank was impressed with everything that he had witnessed to that day. Heather, or his daughter, in his eyes, was certainly doing well considering the life that had been thrown in front of her. The yard, the house, the cooking, the whole atmosphere was a good one to raise children and he could sense happiness in that roomy house.

"Well, who's going to take care of that yard for you now?" Frank questioned Kareen in a sense of repairing things between the two.

"Well, I figured I'd wake up an hour earlier once a week," Kareen answered with a smile. "I would like to apologize for the way I have been acting towards you, Frank," Kareen continued. "You know I didn't have the best impression of you since, ya know, all the stuff I have heard about you, but I can sincerely tell you that I was wrong and I apologize," she finished and Frank was speechless. He had not expected the girl to give him any room to breathe, but was grateful to witness some compassion.

Heather knew what was coming next and it had nothing to do with compassion. She just sat back and ate her food as she watched what she knew was about to transpire before them all. "I can take care of the yard until you guys get some help at the store," Frank offered to Kareen.

"We would love that!" Kareen responded with another overly large smile. She then followed up with another weakening blow. "Kids, tell grandpa what you guys are going to do this summer," she said in Steph and Braylen's direction.

"SOOOOOOCCCCERRRR," the toddlers screamed in unison. Frank was taken aback by the kids' excitement and the word they just screamed. No cheerleader, no football. He was surprised. It was not in the little one's destiny to chase a ball around a field. It was his destiny to score six.

"So you're going to let him play, huh? I can tell this one has already been discussed," Frank questioned Heather and Kareen. The girls could see the obvious disgust in the man's face and it was nothing short of what they expected.

"Yeah," Kareen began, "how would you like to be their coach?"

# PART 24

Silence filled the room and Frank's mind started running in circles. He knew he was trapped into saying yes so he obliged, "Yes, I'll do it, but I don't know the first thing about that sport."

"Well, we can all learn together then. I will sign you up tomorrow when I go into the store. You just have to make sure you pick Braylen and Steph to be on your team when the pool gets drawn," Heather began to explain the details. Frank was listening, but not comprehending what Heather was saying. He just wondered what this new change would bring. He always dreamed of Braylen growing up and replacing his daddy as a star on offense, not one of the scrawny long haired kids on that fairy soccer team. He had never respected the sport, but he knew this would be an opportunity for him to see his grandson more. He came to conclusions in his head that it wouldn't be so bad. He just had a thing or two to learn and it sure would be interesting dealing with a bunch of three to five year olds.

"Dan is going to be your assistant coach," Kareen broke Frank's train of thought. "We discussed it with him today when we let them take over the store." Heather caught the lie, but knew that Frank would never have a clue. He didn't need to know that he had been the target in the situation or what the real motives were.

"Well, looks like you guys had me pinned on this one before I even knew what was happening. You just sort of made your minds up, huh?" Frank prodded for an explanation and Kareen took the opportunity.

"Well, the kids really want to play and you said you're turning your life around. It just makes sense for you to do it. We know you and you want to have a closer bond with your grandson. This will give you an opportunity to get away from that junk yard and spend time with him every day. It just seemed to fit. Don't worry, we did the same exact thing with Dan, except he was a little faster to jump on the idea than you were," Kareen finished her explanation with a short jab in the pinned man's direction.

"Well, since you guys have it all figured out, I think I better get up to speed on it." Frank gave a shy smile as he was turning the idea.

"No worries about that, Frank," Kareen said as she walked into the living room and picked up a book. She brought it into the dining room and sat it down in front of Frank. She then let the kids down so they could wear themselves out before a bath and bedtime.

"Soccer for Dummies?" Frank read aloud with a chuckle. Heather hadn't known about the book and she wondered how long Kareen had planned this. She wasn't going to jump in the way, however, as she knew they needed a united front against Frank to completely persuade him into the coaching position. "Well, I guess this will give me something to do between hauling junk away from the yard and paperwork," Frank said in a merciful tone. He knew for a fact he had been beat. He let his brain get over the idea, however, and actually became excited for the time that he would be spending with Braylen. He had come to rest on the same thoughts as before and knew he would just keep going in circles if he let himself dwell on it, so he decided to just embrace it.

"So when does this all start?" Frank began to dig for information from the two sitting across from him.

"Well, in two days they are pulling all the signup sheets out of the stores and putting the kids' signup sheets in. Monday, you will have a meeting at the city building. I'm not sure of the time. The pull for teams will be two weeks from now." Kareen fulfilled Frank's wishes for information and he asked another question.

"Where do they play at?" It was a question that Kareen had already prepared an answer, as well as a proposal for.

"Well, right now they play in the park. It's a very small field, which is okay for three to five year olds, but for older kids it's just not enough. The high school team has a field as well, but with holes divoting the surface, and has a crazy arc. It was built where the old high school stood," Kareen finished her explanation and Frank could sense that she gave him way too much information for a reason. Heather wondered the same exact thing, as Kareen had went off on the tangent. They hadn't discussed any of this before Frank arrived.

Kareen broke the silence with another stern explanation, "Frank, I was curious one day and drove out by where you live. It's out of the way, but only five minutes from the center of town. I noticed you have a bunch of land out there that has been cleared off, but your junk yard isn't taking up even nearly half of it. Why not build a complex where the kids could play at? I know you have the tractors and dozers and tools for something like that. All you would need for now it a flat piece of land to etch out a couple playing fields and a gravel parking lot. All it would cost you is some time and some land. You know the state is giving out grants for things that will get kids active," Kareen flung her offer on the table and had no idea what Frank's reaction was going to be.

"How did we go from coaching to a whole damn complex in my back yard?" Frank questioned. He was agitated, but could see where the woman was coming from. She was right, but he didn't appreciate the way she just threw everything at him in a manner that blindsided him.

"So I'll propose this to you," Frank began a counter offer, "if you get a grant, I will build the field. I know it won't happen this year, but for the next year. If we are going to do this thing I'm going to have an actual complex with fenced in fields and a paved parking lot. We could throw a baseball and softball part in this as well. We both know that all this county cares about is that football team. Hell, all I care about is that football team, but I know I need to support my grandchild and it would help this community. Furthermore, it would help clear my name. Maybe Elizabeth would take a second look at me after she sees all this get done." The man paused as he was surprised he had let the name slip out of his mouth. Everyone caught it but no one wanted to pry. That was fragile territory and nobody wanted to break that glass. Frank continued to speak again, "I will etch out one field with my grater for now and make a small parking lot. I can probably also weld up a couple goals if I can get blueprints for one. You guys work on getting some sponsors to support the league with nets and such and I'll put a chain link fence on both ends of the field to hang the placards on and stop wild balls."

Frank stopped in the middle of his rant, surprised at just how fast he had come to grip onto this idea. He liked the idea and he liked it a lot. He knew that it would bring a lot of opportunities for his business and, as he had let slip out of his mouth, it may clear him for a second chance with Elizabeth. The girls were blown away and almost had to force their bottom jaw off of the carpet. Here was a man that almost became furious that they had pinned a coaching position on him and now five minutes later he is drawing out a soccer complex in front of them.

"I will write up all the grants tonight after I get the kids asleep, Frank, and bring them over tomorrow after we close the shop. We can review them together as I'm sure you will know more about this than I do," Kareen began an explanation as Heather backed her.

"Yeah, we best apply for all we can get," Heather said, trying to sound like she had some clue as to what was even going on. "We could donate it in Landon's memory." The second sentence silenced everyone.

# PART 25

It was a perfect idea, Heather thought. Landon was a god in that town because of sports, so it was only fitting that he would have his name on a sports complex in the small town.

"That would be just perfect," Frank spoke up, "I don't think there would be any more fitting way to memorialize my son and what he did for this town than to build something like that in his honor. I know the town would get behind that and grants would be easier to obtain that way. It just fits, Heather." He smiled across the table at her.

"Yeah," Kareen said. "it will give it more of a sense of belonging as well. If you think about it, not a lot of people in this town really accept the idea of anything other than football. Landon had such an effect on this town that it only seems fitting that this would draw more people to the fields." Frank was surprised how Kareen was always business, but he understood that she didn't have the same sentimental feel for the situation that he shared with Heather. Kareen never knew Landon, so her looking at things in a business sense was to be expected and it was a good thing.

"I will also talk to my father about this," Heather was stirring another wonderful idea. "Frank, you could build bleachers pretty easily. It wouldn't have to be anything too special. Probably just a couple sets for each field, big enough to fit twenty to thirty people on and benches for the teams. My father's construction firm, I'm sure, could donate the chain link fence and other supplies that you needed. They could also donate some man power, I'm sure. All I'll have to do is smile pretty at daddy and I'll get him to give."

Frank knew that Dan would give in and it would be a major help. Dan had part ownership with one of his brothers over a small construction firm in the area. They did mostly residential work, but worked on larger projects once in a while.

"Well, that is two sponsors," Frank said. "We will need a lot more than that to really get something like this going."

"Make that three," Kareen interjected. "Our little store can supply the items that the concessions will need. Then the money made can go right back into the fields. We will need gas for the mowers and things of that sort."

"Well, looks like we have a plan," Frank said with some enthusiasm. "I will get one of my hands to grade a spot off tomorrow after I get some dimensions tonight. I'll weld up a couple benches and gravel a parking lot and we will go from there."

"Sounds awesome," Heather said with one of her white, all American smiles.

"Well, now that we got this all settled and I was attacked by you couple lions, Imma manage to limp out of this den," Frank said with a smile and found his way to the play room to give the toddlers his goodbyes. He then walked outside the door stopping on the porch to talk a few moments with Heather. "Seriously, Heather, thank you for this opportunity and brushing our differences aside. I wish I never would have put myself in a position as to where I would have to redeem myself, but I plan to make good on my word. I'll be seeing you soon, daughter." The title by which Frank just addressed Heather struck her still in her tracks.

"Daughter," she whispered to herself as he backed out of the drive.

Kareen was behind Heather and slowly reached her arms around the girl's waist. Heather jumped when she felt Kareen's touch.

"Scared me, crazy," she said as she caught the breath she had lost. Kareen gave a small chuckle and placed her head on Heather's shoulder and they both watched the taillights disappear in the darkness. "Looks like we have him right where we want him," Heather said, "but when did you go out to his place to investigate and when did you plan on telling me about this idea. I don't like you sneaking things up on me like that, hun. We're supposed to be a team here," she ended quietly with the pursuing questions. Kareen squeezed her waist a little tighter and began her explanation.

"I didn't really even have that idea, Heather. It just sort of hit me while we were sitting there. I thought it would be an awesome idea and we already had him pinned down . . . I figured we may as well use that chance to kick him a few times."

"Yeah, that makes sense. Just warn me next time," Heather responded.

Kareen gave Heather a small kiss on her neck and the two turned and walked inside. Heather was getting nervous at this point that so much was going right in her life. She just wondered when the Jenga block would be pulled that would make her whole tower fall. She was terrified of it actually, but she wouldn't let the fear ruin the end of her good day. She joined Kareen with the kids in the play room they had. Since Heather had started staying in Kareen's room they had moved everything out of her room. They padded the bottom three feet of the walls in multicolor and the floor as well. It wasn't large, but it was, in a sense, the children's own indoor playground. It was a safe place to leave the kids unsupervised for a few minutes at a time. Both kids were incredibly wound tight this night because they overheard the whole discussion about soccer. Of course, they were too young to comprehend what anything meant besides the words "yes, they could play" and at that age that's all they needed to know anyways.

"Why don't you pick out a bottle of wine and a movie and I'll get the kids ready for bed," Heather offered to Kareen. Kareen obliged and left Heather alone with the children so that she could get them wound down for the night.

"Mommy, is we going to play soccer this year?" Braylen asked Heather in his cute little sincere tone.

"Of course, baby, but not tonight. We have to get you two to sleep. It's too late out for little kids to be awake," Heather answered and was greeted with whimpers from both children. She stopped for a second and looked them both over. Steph was looking more and more every day like Kareen, Heather thought, and Braylen was Landon completely, except for that hair. No one could mistake who that kid's parents were. She grabbed them both by the hand and led them to their room for a bed time story. She read them their favorite bedtime story after she got them dressed down. She knew soon enough that these moments would pass and they would have to split rooms in the next year or so. She read the story and they both slowly drifted off to sleep. Heather waited for a few minutes and then, satisfied that both the children were fast asleep, walked downstairs.

"I pulled out one of the older years for tonight," Kareen greeted Heather from the couch.

"I like the older years. They tend to be sweeter," Heather answered and threw herself onto the couch beside her secret lover. "We accomplished a lot today," Heather said as she poured herself a glass.

"I simply cannot wait to see if Frank backs up his talk," Kareen agreed. She knew in her head that the plans they had laid out today were going to be difficult. "I have to look up grants tonight . . . ugh," Kareen said in a complaining tone.

"We can do it together," Heather said. "Just remember, we are doing this for the kids and that is what makes it worth it," Heather agreed and raised her glass. "Here's to the Landon Maston memorial Sports Complex," she proposed the toast and both the females took a drink from their glass.

"Tomorrow while I'm reviewing the grants with Frank, you need to sweet talk your father with those beautiful blue eyes of yours, Heather," Kareen looked in Heather's direction.

"You have no idea how easy that will be," Heather answered and then gave Kareen a small kiss.

# PART 26

Another week had passed and it was week three of the store being open and the first day that the new hires that Dan interviewed would start. Heather had no idea what she was going to do with a day to herself as her parents were going to watch the children so that the girls could have the day free. Kareen had plans, however.

"Let's go see how the field is coming, babe," Kareen said as she walked into the kitchen. It was three hours past the normal time they woke up, but still relatively early.

"Well, let me drink this cup of coffee and we can go," Heather responded.

"Girl, put it in a cup and bring it with you. I'm anxious to go check out what Frank does," Kareen responded. "Hell, you look just fine in those sweats and a ponytail anyways." Heather knew that when Kareen was in this mood she was better off to just comply with the request, so she did as instructed, poured the coffee into a foam cup, and headed out towards the car where Kareen was waiting.

"What's that?" Heather questioned. Kareen was wrestling a box into the hatch of the small car.

"The soccer nets came in the mail today, babe. You didn't think I just got excited for nothing, did you? Practice starts three days from now. They almost didn't make it in time." Heather smiled and walked over to help Kareen out.

"Girl you're like a little kid before Christmas with this stuff," Heather teased.

"Well, to be honest with you, I love the idea of being a soccer mom and not the 'oh, she's hot' part, just the whole world the athletic part brings. I was never really given a chance to be athletic as a kid, so I've always wanted that healthy lifestyle for my own," Kareen responded to the small jab.

"Well, I guess ninety minutes of running around is pretty athletic," Heather responded.

"Well, you mean two twenty minute halves for our children," Kareen corrected.

"Oh, my bad," Heather said with a smile as she sat down in the small car. The two then pulled out of the driveway and headed to Frank's.

First, they decided to stop at the small store and see how things were going. The two teenagers inside seemed to be keeping things alright. They agreed to start out at seven dollars an hour as long as they kept their grades in school over a "B" average. It was Dan's idea to keep a small incentive and standard so that they could get quality kids to work there. They knew that if the children had a "B" average or above, they would most likely be more responsible and able to handle the small problems that came along with the small store.

"Kareen," one of the workers called from the grill, "where do you keep the salt? I couldn't find any at all, so I took some of the shelf. I hope that's alright," the teenager further explained.

"That's definitely coming out of your paycheck," Kareen said in a stern voice. The worker looked like a whipped puppy. "I'm just kidding. It will be fine. I think we were out of the commercial stuff anyways," Kareen responded and the teenager blushed.

"Feel free to make your own decisions. We wouldn't let you work here if you weren't smart kids," Heather directed to both, then looking at the kid behind the cash register. "How are things looking today?"

"Well, we're a little slow today, but it's probably good, being it's our first day alone in here," the girl responded.

"Yeah, you guys seem like you have the hang of things, though," Heather said as she grabbed another cup of coffee

"Yeah, I guess. It's sort of interesting to hear the people that come in off the interstate talk. You know there are some very different people that come in here, Heather," the girl explained. Heather gave a small chuckle.

"Well, we are going to get out of your guys' hair. You have control here," Heather responded, picked up her coffee off the counter, and walked out the door with Kareen following closely behind.

"Well, it looks like Dan picked a pretty good set to take over for us," Kareen offered the encouragement.

"Yeah," Heather began, "I had never heard of the whole 'B' average thing or anything like that, but you know what? For the few dollars we are paying them over minimum wage, I think it's definitely worth it. They picked up extremely fast and are already making wise decisions on their own." Heather paused and then gave a brief example to back up her explanation, "You know, any other kid would have just said, 'Hell with it,' and probably just left salt out of everything until we arrived to give them direction." Kareen knew exactly what Heather was saying and agreed.

"Yeah, your right, babe. I was completely shocked when he told me that he had taken the initiative to do something like that."

Heather clicked the knob of the radio on and the two continued their journey to the fields.

No more than ten minutes later, Frank's residence and the fields came into view. The first very noticeable difference was the graded and freshly graveled driveway heading up to Frank's and then forking off to the fields on the left about a half mile further. Heather could see things were taking shape at a highly rapid rate. One field had already been graded and a set of bleachers placed on both sides. It was incomplete and missing some things, but the grass seed was already blooming a bright green and it looked peaceful up on top of the roaming hills.

"Well, look at that," Heather whispered as her eyes came across a new discovery. Frank was on top of one of his old rusty graders and he was etching out another pair of fields beside where the full side field was. These fields were half size and they already had goals pushed off to the sides for the extra fields.

"Good thing I bought a couple extras and different sizes," Kareen followed up Heather's whisper. "Looks like Frank is going one step above everything and decided to go past one field," Kareen said. Looking further into things as they parked Heather noticed that her dad's construction firm was already out there setting fence posts around the entirety of the larger field and not just around the goals like had been discussed. "Looks like your dad is going one step further, too," Kareen whispered back to Heather as the two females stepped out of the car.

The place was coming together, Heather thought to herself. It was just an imaginary image only three weeks prior and now here it was in front of her. She saw now that Frank really was trying to prove a point to everyone with the making of this new complex for the kids. She was further surprised when five sprinklers began to spray their share of water over the fresh growing grass.

"Well," Kareen said as she jumped out of the way of some of the water, "let's go talk to the mastermind behind all this." The two leisurely walked over as Frank hopped down from the rusty old machinery with a smile. Dan spotted the visitors and started heading in their direction as well.

"Well, what do you think?" the guys questioned almost in unison, already knowing by the look on the two girls' faces that they were thoroughly surprised.

"Well, I definitely have to apologize for doubting you, Frank," Heather responded.

"So just how far are you planning to go with this right now?" Kareen questioned.

"Catch us up," Heather added with a smile. The four of them gingerly walked towards one of the new sets of bleachers and sat down to discuss how everything was going.

"Well," Frank began, "I know we only discussed starting out with one field, but I thought about it and it's just not likely we would be able to give each team enough practice time to do them any good with just one field. I looked at the signup sheets and talked to the principal of the high school. The school's athletic boosters are going to supply the scoreboard if we let the high school team play here."

"That's why I'm adding a higher fence behind the goals and fencing the entire larger field off," Dan added.

"Well, what about the sprinklers? Who's funding that water bill?" Kareen said with a laugh.

"Well, that's coming off the spout at my shop," Frank said. "I dug a line from there to here and I will just write it off on taxes at the end of the year. It's really no big deal. You have no idea how much better the grass will grow if it's watered daily," Frank finished. "The smaller fields will be for the little kids to play on. Instead of putting more than one set of lines on the larger field, each level has a separate field."

"We made two smaller ones because we knew we would have a lot of younger kids in the league," Dan further explained. Kareen hopped up and jogged over to the car getting the box out.

"You want to help hang these?" she asked in the other three's direction. They obliged and began the task with smiles.

# PART 27

A week later and practice began. The younger kids practice in the evening before the high school kids' second practice. It was hectic, but only one field had been left alone with enough time for the grass to grow and the two smaller fields were seeding, but not quite ready yet. Frank had already made plans to cut the fields for the kids to practice on. One small field and one large field were mowed in a few days and that was good enough to make up the practice fields. Frank was truly treating it like his own professional complex and he was proud of the work he had been able to complete with a man that had, at one time, broken his nose. The grant had also come through at a fast rate due to some connections with the governor of the state and the baseball and softball diamonds were taking shape as well. The whole place was designed in the shape of a horseshoe with the game fields at one end, two fields in the middle, and the practice fields on the other end. A gravel parking lot would be added in the center of it all.

There was a new buzz around town about it all. Some of it was good and some of it was bad. The older men could be overheard talking at the little store. "Why would Frank build something like that in memory of a sport that his son didn't play?" was just one of the statements that could be overheard on a typical morning. The truth was Frank knew things were changing. Things had changed in his life and were probably going to change in that small town as well. The only other time that town had even toyed with the idea of anything to do with soccer was when the women's team won the world cup in '91. Even then, it only lasted that following summer and only extended to the girls. Frank had grown used to the idea of it catching on in the small town and being more than a "nerd" sport. He knew that with this sport he could dedicate it to the memory of his son without the pain of reliving every Friday night. At any rate, either good or bad, it had grown up fast and it was getting utilized. Seventy-three kids had signed up that year from ages three to fourteen. Not a bad turn-out for a football diseased town.

Both Frank and Dan had read the prescribed "Soccer for Dummys" book, but the duo looked lost out on the field. It was quite a comical sight to see them try to set up the drills for the toddlers to run through. At that young age, all the kids wanted to do anyways was just group around the ball and kick at it until it moved three feet and repeat again. The concept that the adults were trying to grasp was as farfetched as ever. The men gave up after first few days, however, and grasped the fact that kids were going to do what they wanted at that age no matter what they were taught. It was better to take the win factor out of everything, anyways, at that age. It would give them a chance to learn just as much as the kids. All they really had to do was teach them which goal to kick the ball into and not to use their hands. It was a simple enough concept. For a child three to five years in age, not picking up that ball and running with it is quite the accomplishment.

The few weeks of initial practice had gone by fast and the complex was already taking larger shape as well. Light poles had been run and the town was going to cover the lighting bill for the fields. It was one of the only fields in their region that could hold night time games as well. Foundations were being laid for bathrooms, a concession stand, and bleachers with a fence around the whole complex. The high school team had also seen a larger turnout as well and their season had already started. Many compliments were given on the condition of the field compared to previous seasons when they played on the school field: "A good field surface makes for better practice which makes for a better team. Hell, on that old pitch with the divots and rocks and such the kids couldn't read the path of the ball. Now they have a grasp. We should win some this year." An excerpt from the coach in the town's overview of the upcoming sports gave thanks to Frank and Dan for the work they had done on the new complex and getting it ready for play. Frank and Dan had grown a bond through the process as well. It was good to get each away from their normal "work schedule" and into something different. It was good for the children as well to see a united front when they looked to their sets of grandparents.

A week into the high school season, it was their third game and first home game. It would be a large event for the town, not because of the sport, but because of the memorial that was being dedicated to the family and children connected to Landon. They had named the complex after him. It was on the signs on the road and on a small statue in front of the now standing concession stand. The statue of Landon catching that game winning state tournament touchdown pass looked a little off in the middle of a soccer/softball/baseball complex but everyone knew who Landon was and that was who they knew him as. Nothing would have been more fitting.

Both teams warmed up for the game and the bleachers were packed due to the dedication ceremony that would soon commence. Before the game, a podium was placed out on the center of the largest field and a ceremony took place. Elizabeth, Frank, Lisa, Dan, and Heather all stood behind as the mayor gave a small speech. She finished with her normal talk about what sports meant to that community and it was the families' turn.

Heather was first at the podium. She talked of what it would have meant to Landon to see that many people turn out for something to do with sports. She told them of his secret love for the game and that he probably would have chosen soccer instead of football had the team been successful and it was accepted at the time. It was true. Even though Landon was a god known for football, he was good at almost every sport he played at the school. He was also on the basketball team and baseball team as well. Lastly, she challenged everyone to embrace, instead of push away, the complex and the new sports that in the near future could grow in the town. Everyone applauded as Heather resided to her place with the rest of the family while Frank and Dan walked up to the podium.

"We would like to welcome Kareen Thomas up here as well," Frank said into the microphone and everyone watched as Kareen shyly walked her way to the field. They pulled Heather up to their sides as well.

"We did the work," Frank began, "but none of this would have even been thought of if it wasn't for these two wonderful young women by my side. A month ago, Heather called me up and invited me to dinner," Frank paused and chuckled to himself as he remembered the incidents. "Let's just say these ladies fattened me up and then pushed me into a corner for this. Now I can honestly say we hated this idea, but you do what you do for your kids and, in this case, our grandchildren. These ladies took it one step further and pushed us to do it for a whole community," Frank finished and the town people rose and gave them an ovation.

"Landon was a great man that blessed me with a wonderful grandchild, but I would like for you all to know this was built just as much for you as it was for him," Dan said after the applause simmered. The statue was unveiled and it was time for the game to begin.

The majority of the people that had come to watch the dedication stayed to watch the game as it had already taken up the majority of their evening anyway. Steph and Braylen were so excited to watch the "Big Kids' play. Dan, Frank, Elizabeth, Lisa, Heather, and Kareen all grouped together on the bleacher to root on the home team. None of them had even watched a soccer game on T.V. before, let alone in real life. Frank and Dan began to converse in the first few minutes of the game over how much actual control there was in the chaos. They noticed that a pair of tall kids were playing the striker position. That pair of tall kids were supposed to make it in the starting lineup this year in football as a twin threat, but had opted to play soccer. It was a beginning to a big change that would take place in that small community. The crowd in attendance was granted a fast paced physical game. Instead of a bunch of fairies running around, they saw athletes mixed in with the nerds. The game was winding down and it looked as if it was going to end in a tie. Frank couldn't believe it. Ninety minutes of running up and down and it was going to end in a tie? One of the tall forwards broke his train of thought, however, as he began to streak down the side with a little one, two triangle pass with the other striker. The kid took it to the corner of the field granting confusion to the whole soccer illiterate town, but an answer came as the kid booted a floater to the center of the field. The other forward received the ball at the eighteen yard box, let the ball take a bounce, and blasted it into the bottom corner of the net. Shortly after the goal, the referee called full time. It was fitting. The first win in school history came on the day of the dedication.

# PART 28

As the game ended and the celebration began, everyone stood up and began to clap for the home team. Out of excitement, Heather looked over at Kareen and placed a soft brief kiss on her partner's lips. A look of astonishment found its way onto the girl's face. It was brief compared to their previous encounters with romance which were occurring nightly now, but this one was in public.

"What was that?" she mouthed in her direction, and another "What the hell was that?" was thrown in from Lisa. Heather realized what she had done. Nobody except for Kareen and Heather knew about the secret, but it was out now.

"Oh I'm just so happy! The excitement got the best of me," Heather said in an attempt to dim down the situation. She could feel all eyes were on her and holes were being stared through her tiny little body. She didn't offer any explanation, just grabbed Braylen by the hand and pulled him onto the field. She stood there kicking a ball with her overjoyed toddler. Kareen quickly followed.

"Do you know what you just did?" Kareen questioned Heather with a sense of urgency.

"Yes . . . I mean . . . I don't know," Heather stammered around. A feeling of guilt crept over her. She wondered how many people saw that kiss and how their opinions of her would change. But, on the other hand she knew she wouldn't be able to hide it forever and to hell with what they say anyways. She felt she didn't owe anyone anything. She had built a life by herself with the help of Kareen and she was able to make her own decisions.

"You will have to do some explaining, you know that, Heather," Kareen began to prod further. Kareen knew that Heather had no clue of the ramifications that this would hold. Kareen came to the town as an outsider and from that angle she was able to better figure out what was accepted and what was not. The two girls were fooling around in an area that was highly thought of against. Neither knew, however, what it could cause.

"Well, I was just excited," Heather began. "You're the one I turn to always. You're my good morning kiss and my goodnight kiss. It's just habit." Kareen thought the explanation was adorable, but knew that they were going to need a lot more than adorable if anybody outside the realm of their family caught that brief lesbian encounter.

"It's ok, babe. Nothing we can do about it now," Kareen offered some encouragement, "but where do you plan to go with it from here? What are we going to tell everyone if questions get asked? I know your mother saw it, so your, I mean, our family is going to question things, but what do we tell them?" Kareen questioned. Heather paused for a brief moment to try to let everything sink in. She wondered how she could explain it to everyone in a manner in which would cause the least amount of back blast. What way could she tell everyone that they could just brush it off and not think twice about what they had just seen?

She wanted to hide it and blame it on excitement, but she knew it was an affair that wasn't ending anytime soon. She felt if she didn't cover it up it would be easier to deal with in the long run, but at the same time she didn't want to deal with this mess right now when everything was going so well. Kareen could once again spot that vein popping out on Heather's temple.

"What are you thinking about inside that head of yours?" Kareen tried to lighten the situation as she gave Heather a playful shove. She knew that Heather was swimming inside an ocean of thoughts inside her brain. She was wearing floaties in a pool of Olympic proportions. Kareen attempted to slow it all down for her now not so secret lover. "Babe, just calm down," she said as she kicked a ball back to the two children. "No matter what they think or what goes on, we still have each other and our children. None of these people, not even your parents, provide us with anything that we have."

Heather knew that she was right and she figured she would just blow it off for now if at all possible. "Yeah, babe . . . ." she said as she kicked a ball in Braylen's direction. The four continued to play as Lisa walked towards them. Lisa had that familiar smile on her face. The one that meant that she had something on her mind, but was trying to put up a front.

"So . . . uh, good game, huh? That was a treat. I've never even seen that sport played before. I'm used to the Friday Night Lights. This was certainly a different sort of athleticism I witnessed today. You guys really did a good thing here with this field, girls. You work together awesome as a pair, but the thing I want to know is what type of pair am I looking at?" Lisa ended what appeared to be a normal gratifying conversation with a mind numbing question. Heather wanted to act as if she hadn't caught the question and just continue kicking the ball. She looked at her mother as she dug for the answer. She knew that she wouldn't get out of that place without presenting something decent in her mother's direction. Something that her brain could fill this void on and make everything that Lisa just witnessed normal.

It was an impossible task to please Lisa with any sort of answer, though, and Heather began, "I was just excited, mother. No big deal."

"How it is no big deal? There were a ton of people here that could have witnessed that little encounter. How do you think your father feels and how do you think Frank and Elizabeth look at you? You possibly changed hundreds of ways people will look at you guys now and what would it mean for those children?" Lisa was throwing piercing questions in Heather's direction and the girl was frozen in the line of fire.

"Well, mom, you're taking it way too damn far here. I was just excited and I'm comfortable with Kareen. It's not like I laid her down and ripped her clothes off in front of everyone. We didn't do anything that you couldn't witness on the damn TV, mother. I'm not a fucking lesbian or anything! It was a small peck. Hell, I still kiss you and daddy like that," Heather came out with her own guns blazing. Lisa was used to the girl that was inside her daughter three years ago, not this woman now pressing things back in her direction.

"Well, look at you talking like you're all fucking grown. I'm your mother, Heather. You will address me with respect." It was only the second or third time in Heather's life that she had her mother say the "F" word. She knew she had pushed some buttons, but she couldn't find a reason to even care. Her mother walked across the field and to her vehicle. The conversation was far from over, but she knew that the way things were looking she would probably lay hands on her daughter. Heather was astonished that her mother walked away without a fight. She had never seen her mother so furious in her life and she knew that this snowball would eventually turn into an avalanche. She brushed it away for the time being. For her son's sake, she didn't want the clueless toddler knowing there was anything going on. His world for now was a utopia and she didn't want that to change anytime soon. She reached down and hugged him as she took a deep breath. He pulled away and kicked the ball in Kareen's direction. Heather rose back up straight and caught a reassuring smile from Kareen. She walked over and put her arm around the girl's shoulder. Kareen knew exactly what was about to be coming down their lane, but she figured they could handle it. The two stood side by side and watched as the kids played. They stayed there until the parking lot cleared out and the lights were kicked off.

"Time to go home," Kareen whispered to Heather.

"Yeah, let's go . . . ." Heather answered and her voice trailed off.

## PART 29

No one had really witnessed the kiss except for Heather's mother. At least that was what Heather had wished the lack of talk around town had meant. Surely, if people had seen it, somebody would say something. She would be the talk of town. The old ladies would whisper while in her store and look away at her glances. But, none of that was happening, and she was glad. Instead, things went as normal. The kids were still enthralled about soccer, and their first game was today. She knew that the excitement on them was overbearing and watched both proudly pull their tiny soccer shirts on before they headed to the field. Their laughter and excitement carried the car to the fields. Heather followed her normal habit of striving never to be early. Kareen and some of the other parents were already waiting by the time she pulled up. She put the car in park and pulled both the children out of the back seat. They took off for the field as she walked in Kareen's direction.

"How are you doing, momma?" Kareen said as Heather walked up. Kareen was in a maroon track suit with her hair pulled back in a pony tail. She was absolutely gorgeous, Heather thought to herself and had to collect her thoughts before addressing the good morning.

"Well, how were things this morning?" she asked Kareen, referencing the opening of the store and getting things ready for the game. The four hired kids ran the store weeknights and weekend days and did it quite well.

"Well, everything went well as always . . . what about with you." Kareen replied. It was awkward compared to their normal good morning conversations. Heather did not like waking up without Kareen by her side, but she knew a day like this it was normal. She wanted more than anything to just wrap her arms around her partner and give her one of the deep, time stopping kisses, but fought off the urge and continued on her walk. She walked over and checked the concession stand with Kareen following.

"So you gotta double check all my work?" Kareen said as they walked through the door. Heather didn't know Kareen was following her, but took the opportunity to get what she was wanting earlier. She wrapped her arms around Kareen's waist and pulled her in for a deep kiss making sure to lightly bite Kareen's lips as she finished. "Yeah, I could read that look on your face," Kareen said with a slightly turned on smile.

"Oh, yeah?" Heather said as she pulled away. "You just think you know everything don't you?" She shot Kareen a playful smile and began to open the shutters to let the cool summer morning's air on them both. "Well, how do you think today is going to go?" Heather questioned as she opened the last window.

"I don't know. I figure we will see a bunch of kids running around chasing a ball. Cute, to say the least," Kareen said. Glancing out the window, she caught Dan and Frank pulling into the parking lot. They had arrived in the same vehicle. These small town people sure do get over grudges fast, she thought to herself as she walked accompanied by Heather to their direction.

"Hello, Daddy," Heather said as she gave Dan a hug and a kiss on the cheek.

"Well, hello, pumpkin," he said in return, almost in shock. It had been forever since his daughter had walked up to him and greeted him in that way. He missed knowing he was the center of her world and cherished the small moment she had just granted him.

"Well, looks like you have things going pretty well. I had one of my hands come up here at six to mow and bag the fields before today's events. I love this fresh smell of grass and the cool air," Frank began to explain. He was a changed man from the time that he lost Landon and he was glad he was able to show the world. He knew second chances were almost never granted, and was thankful for the second chance he had here. A lot of time and effort had gone into the field, but he felt everything in front of him was worth it. The place was paying for itself with the concession stand and the admission and all he had to do was pay his hands a little extra for the field care. They had laughed at the idea at first, but it's not often someone turns down money for small jobs.

Frank parted the group with a smile and walked to the smaller fields to pull the sprinklers off. It had seeded extremely well, just as the larger one had, and they even mowed the token plaid pattern in it as well, just like the larger one. In his opinion, his practice fields were even better than most game fields.

"Well, who are we going to start today?" Dan said as he approached Frank's side.

"I haven't thought about it," Frank said as he got lost in thought. He was surprised by the question.

"I thought about this last night and I think I have the perfect idea," Dan explained and Frank slowed the pace of the walk to show that Dan had his attention.

"Well, go on," Frank said.

"I think we should run this by the parents and they will understand completely. We're dealing with 3 to 5 year olds here, so sure it would be nice to win, but it's not a priority of mine. We both know this game is just going to be them chasing the ball around anyways."

"You don't have to sell it to me, man. Just tell me the plan," Frank interrupted with a chuckle.

"Well, as I was saying, I brought the old wheel they use for bingo and wrote the kids names on the balls. Every day before the game we will roll the wheel in front of them to pick the players that will start that day. It eliminates all ideas of favoritism and it seems completely fair and honest," Dan finished and realized he did sound like he was trying to throw a sales pitch in Frank's direction.

"I think that sounds like a pretty darn good idea," Frank said when he knew that Dan was finished. The two finished pulling the sprinklers off the field and it was time for the teams to start warming up. A few people had strolled in casually to watch the early afternoon game and some members of the Baptist church had stayed back as well from the practice they held on the field. It was another one of Frank's newly good deeds, letting the church use the softball field for their tournaments and such.

"This place is gaining popularity faster than I ever thought it would," Dan admitted as the two looked around.

"Yeah, looking back six months ago, this was all just a random idea in those two crazy girls' heads." Frank let out another one of his healthy chuckles.

The kids started warming up, and comments of how nice the complex was rang out from the opposing team's parents. As always, Frank and Dan beamed with pride over hearing yet another round of acceptance into the community from outsiders and insiders alike. Before the game, the coaches pulled the parents together and explained to them Dan's idea with the bingo wheel. It was accepted unanimously as a fair way to choose and they carried out the pickings. Braylen was in the starting line-up, but Steph was not. Dan felt bad, but knew that there would be times that this would be the complete opposite and knew he couldn't show favoritism to his grandkids. The game started and it was just what everyone knew it would be. The positions that the kids were picked to be placed in flew to the way side and the constant giggles and enthusiasm replaced them. About five minutes in, Dan watched a familiar car pull up. Elizabeth got out and walked over to the field, taking a place beside Lisa, Heather, and Kareen.

"She came," Dan heard Frank whisper and looked over to see a beaming smile on the man's face.

## PART 30

Its struck Dan as odd why Frank would be so excited to see Elizabeth at that game, after all Braylen was her grandson, too. He didn't know of Frank's plans to get Elizabeth back. The man had been able to grab every part of his life back except for his love. Elizabeth had left Frank because of the alcohol and how he treated Landon. Frank always had a temper when he was drinking which had seemed like a daily reoccurrence. But the man had been sober for over two years now and he was really getting his life on track. To his knowledge, Elizabeth had never been serious with anyone else. She had the occasional boyfriend here and there, but nothing, Frank thought, that should get in his way. He had planned to ask her out after the game. He figured there was almost no way she could say no if he asked her if she wanted to take Braylen and Steph out for ice cream. With a sober mind, he was able to scrounge up the craftiest ideas and this would be one of them.

Frank grabbed a hold of his wandering attention and brought it back to the game. Braylen, at three years old, seemed to have more of a grasp for the game than even the five year olds. For the age group, he was impressive the way he would just barge his way through a pile and come out with the ball bouncing in front of him. He didn't have any sort of ball control or anything; it just seemed the ball was always at his feet. Frank couldn't help but think how good of a running back he could have been. He knew that almost six sense for the ball was only given to gifted and natural athletes, but once again his brain told him he just needed to support his grandchild. One of the kids broke his train of thought as he kicked the ball all of ten yards and it rolled past the opposing team's goalie. The small kids were elated instantaneously and so were the two coaches. Frank turned and gave Dan a high five and was surprised at how excited he had gotten over this new game.

That was the happiest Dan had seen Braylen in his three year existence. The joy on his grandson's face easily stretched to his. He felt bad for the other team of children as they moped back to their positions for the restart of the game, but knew that he would have to get used to seeing that out of his own team at some point. The game started again and the kids bunched around the ball again. This went on for minutes, with both teams just swarming around the ball.

"Looks like a swarm of angry honeybees around a hive," Frank said with a laugh. It was a perfect figurative example, Dan thought to himself.

"Yeah, and any minute one of 'em will pop out with the ball, legs going hundred miles an hour trying to control the ball, till the others catch up to them and swarm around the ball again." They both shared a laugh and Braylen showed the truth in Dan's statement as he popped out of the pile with the ball about fifteen yards from the other team's goal. He took a couple rather controlled touches and kicked the ball. From eight yards out, the ball hit the back of the net in the air. The kids ran around him in celebration as they had the previous scorer just ten minutes before.

"I don't know if that was luck, but for three, that was a hell of a kick," Dan said in Frank's direction.

"Yeah, at any rate, even if it was luck, I'm sure the coach of the high school team liked the looks of that. He even got a couple controlled touches on it, if you noticed," Frank replied. Both of them were once again blown away with excitement watching how happy the kids were.

"Well, you know Heather says this is all he does when he's got free time outside. Just like Landon, he has that work ethic at such a young age. I know it's early to say, and we both would love to see him play football instead, but there may be something here for him." Dan's statement quieted Frank for a moment. Landon's name still caught him off guard at times, but he realized that Dan was right. Landon had a work ethic and passion in everything that he loved. Frank felt a sense of guilt fall over him. In the midst of all the excitement, he wished he had just once told his son, "good job," instead of, "you can do it better."

"Good job, kid," Frank yelled to Braylen and gave him a thumbs up. He knew this time he would have to act differently. He regretted dearly the moments he had pushed Landon instead of loved him. He wished he could have told Landon how he really felt about him before that incident or be there to take that bullet for him. He was smacked in the face with the fact that life is tough and second chances were not always granted. He lost his son that day and it changed the rest of his life. Now, he was standing with a fluorescent green shirt on coaching the squires. If you would have asked him years ago what he would be doing in four years, he would probably have called you a slur of words from behind a dirty mustache with a muddy thought process. Life changes in a second and changes people. "That's crazy," Frank whispered.

"I know it is," Dan answered with no clue that Frank was talking about a mess inside of his own head instead of the jubilation on the field.

The game started back up again with ten minutes left. The coaches felt good that their first endeavor in this position would end in a win. They knew it was most likely luck, but that didn't matter. A win was a win, no matter what age group. They knew that they would rather be going home with kids that were winners instead of dealing with the moping toddlers over a loss. Out of the migrating beehive that had once again became what was called a soccer match, one of the kids from the opposing team broke loose and managed to get a goal at almost point blank range. The opposing team's spirits were lifted and the home teams dropped just a little.

"That's good," Dan said under his breath not wanting to let Frank hear what he was thinking, but Frank heard anyways.

"Yeah, I agree. I want to win as much as the rest, but they needed to get at least a goal so that they didn't go home crushed. Hell, only three minutes left, we're going to win anyways," Frank said.

Three minutes passed and the ref ended the game. All the kids on both teams had gotten to play about an equal amount of time. Frank and Dan had managed to work things out fair, as they knew how parents get protective over children at such a young age. They also managed to win. Their team was elated and so were the parents. The kids lined up and slapped hands and then ran to their goal to get a pep talk from their coaches. Looking in from outside you would have thought that they just one the Olympics.

Frank and Dan were hooked at that moment with so much happiness surrounding them. "Well coach, let's go talk to the team," Dan said with the same smile that had been on his face the whole game.

"Yeah, let's do that coach," Frank said. His brain was multi-tasking. He was taking in all the excitement in front of him, but at the same time the ideas he had experienced earlier were creeping back into his brain. He watched Elizabeth as she talked with Kareen and Heather. She was absolutely beautiful in his eyes.

# PART 31

He just wanted to get the pep talk over with and let the kids go. He had a question to ask and he was as nervous now as he had been the first time he asked her out almost thirty years prior when they had gone to school in this same small town. She was the missing piece to the new puzzle he was putting together and he knew he didn't deserve a chance, but merely prayed to God, that if there was a God, he would get some compassion now. He needed something more to prove that all of this change was worth everything he was doing. Step by step, everything had fallen in place, but the one thing he was missing was his immediate family. He would never be able to get Landon back, but he could at least get Elizabeth back. She had to see the change and she had to believe he was different. Or so he wished at least, and on the wishing aspect, his fears of "what if" shot back into his head.

"Come on, man," Dan called in his direction.

The kids were all huddled in a circle by one goal with the parents perched behind them listening for instructions. A smile was perched upon everyone's face and Frank caught himself falling weak as he looked around and his gaze rested on Elizabeth.

"When is the next practice coach?" Dan questioned Frank.

"Well, errrr, ummm . . . Tuesday?" Frank blurted out as he had been caught off guard, lost like a child in the woods in swarming oaks of thoughts.

"This is Tuesday," Dan said.

"Well, two days from now at 6," Frank corrected himself.

"Arrrrreee you sure?" Dan said, drawing every word in the sentence out making the kids laugh.

"Well, yeah. I was just meaning, Tuesday would be the day we win and that's exactly what we did we won," Frank said trying to cover his tracks.

"Now you guys take tomorrow off and get rested up. We have to keep practicing hard like we do if you guys want to win like today. You all did an awesome job," Dan said releasing the children.

Dan pulled Frank off to the side as the kids began to filter out. "You alright, man? You were kind of spacey there on me. You normally know exactly the times and dates," Dan questioned.

"Yeah, I just have some things I really need to do, man. Just some things weighing on my mind lately," Frank answered.

"Well, I mean, I know we didn't get off to the best start with everything, but I have seen you make those changes you needed to change. I'm sure whatever it is, you will get it worked out as you always do," Dan offered encouragement.

"So you think she will take me back?" Frank questioned. Dan was caught off guard. He knew that this was probably what had been weighing on Frank's mind, but he didn't think the guy standing beside him would ever humble himself enough to talk about his problems with anyone. He had seen the changes, but never really adjusted to them completely. He searched inside his head for an answer that would be the best to warrant the question that had been thrown in his direction.

"Well, I mean, I don't really know a lot about you guys," Dan began.

"Bullshit! You know why she left me, Dan. In this small town, everyone knows everything." It was true. Dan knew exactly the reasons why Elizabeth had left Frank. She left him because he was a train wreck of a man. He fell off with the alcohol after his own father had committed suicide. After he picked up the bottle, he never set it down. It was too much for Elizabeth to bear and was not healthy to raise a child around. Elizabeth took her child and ran as far as she could in a small town.

"Yeah, I mean, I know that she left you because of the alcohol," Dan submitted to Frank's accusations. "But you know, women are crazy, man. Who am I to say what decisions she will make? I do know you have made changes in your life and that there is a chance. You just have to make the decision whether or not you're going to let pride stand in the way. All she can really do in the end, though, is say 'no.' No real physical damage."

Frank knew that Dan was right. He was just searching for some sort of confidence boost. The first time he had asked Elizabeth on that date to the dance all those years ago he had done it on a dare and he had friends backing him then. He wished for a second he could turn back the rusty hands of time and pull at least a sample of the absent minded cockiness he had carried as a shield with him as a teenage boy for this now.

"Well, I guess you're right. All she can do is say, 'no,'" Frank responded to Dan's encouragement. The response was almost a confidence booster for him just as much as it was filler for the conversation.

"It's going to be alright, man. I'm sure even if she says no you will get her to give in eventually," Dan offered more encouragement and it was exactly what Frank was looking to hear. He knew it in his head. He just wanted someone to tell him that it would be ok.

"Thanks, man," Frank said with a smile, gave Dan a pat on the back, and began walking in Elizabeth's direction.

"Elizabeth," Frank called ahead as he jogged in her direction. She had already seen the look in his eyes during that pep talk he was giving the kids. She had known that it meant that there was a hurricane going on inside that head of his.

"Yes?" she answered in a tone that was neither inviting nor threatening. She truly was curious about what he would have to say.

"Would you like to take the kids to celebrate with ice cream?" he asked in an almost childish plea. She knew exactly what he had meant by that as he used the same pathetic tone he had the first time he asked her out. She had seen him making changes and she knew he was different. She wanted to learn more about this new man that had broken her heart with a broken bottle before, but she wouldn't give in so easy. She wanted to put up a front, but at the same time she wanted to run into his arms and feel the comfort a man can bring. She decided to extend the conversation instead to test and make sure she knew exactly what was budding in the garden of her ex-husbands ex-alcoholic mind.

"Have you asked Kareen and Heather if we could kidnap their kids for awhile?" Elizabeth prodded further. Frank turned a light shade of red. In his youthful shyness of new love, which was old love, he had forgotten to ask anybody anything. He tried to play it off.

"Well, I figured you would be the hardest one to convince it was a good idea, so I decided it was a good idea to ask you first. I didn't, you know, want to ask them and then show up with Steph and Braylen and have to explain that I got shot down." Elizabeth had bit on his cover up.

"Well, they are my grandkids. You don't honestly think I would turn you down on spending time with them. After all, it is only an ice cream date." She hid some things of her own like how curious she was. Something about the clear look in his eyes that she had known before his drinking days and now sucked her right in. Frank called to the children and they came running over. He knelt down beside them.

"Why don't you two go ask your mommies if Gran Gran and Pap can take you to get ice cream?" The children squealed in excitement and did as they were told. Frank stood up and caught the smile on Elizabeth's face. He knew he was in and decided to push it. "So, who loves on that body of yours now days?" he asked. Her smile only grew bigger and in those few seconds her brain began to erupt in the illusions and claps that fireworks bring. The butterflies were released. She didn't know whether to cave in or push away.

## PART 32

The kids ran screaming back with Heather following. "What time are you going to drop off the monkeys tonight?" Heather said with a smile.

"What time is it now?" Frank said as he looked at his watch. "Six? So, uh, how about we will make sure to have 'em home by nine-thirty?" he finished his statement.

"Good game today, huh?" Heather said making small talk. She wasn't used to seeing Elizabeth and Frank together at all. She knew that Elizabeth was getting lonely without a man in her life and wondered if she had become vulnerable to Frank's advances. They talked for a few moments about the game and about Braylen's goal and it was apparent that Frank was growing impatient about leaving just as much as the kids were.

"I'm going to go get the car seats," Frank said as he turned away from the conversation and headed for Heather's car.

"Well . . . ." Heather began to speak, but Elizabeth cut her off.

"What was I supposed to do tell him? No?" Elizabeth questioned.

"I didn't say anything," Heather began with a smile. "You are a grown woman and you can handle yourself. Besides, you guys are just going to get ice cream, right?" Heather asked a prodding question, already knowing the answer. She knew what Frank was up to and Elizabeth did as well. The whole ice cream thing was just his way of covering up all his boyish intentions in case he got shot down.

"I know, Heather. I'm sorry. I just . . . . I don't . . ." Elizabeth was searching for words as Frank walked back, a booster seat in each arm.

"Why don't ya help me out with this thing? I have no idea how the new ones with all the gizmos work," Frank said and the girls were diverted away from their conversation. They began to laugh as he struggled to put the first one in Elizabeth's SUV. Frank eventually succeeded but after the ladies had already put the other one in. Frank stood up and began to walk away.

"Where are you going?" Elizabeth asked and Frank turned around.

"Well, I, uh, I was going to meet you there," he said shyly, realizing how absurd he sounded. He tried to regain some of the confidence in his voice. "I didn't think you would want someone like me in your vehicle." Elizabeth could see through the shield he was trying to place in front of himself.

"Get your ass in the car," she said with a smirk. Frank was taken aback by the orders his ex-wife had just given.

"No cussing in front of the young'ins, lady," he said as he opened the door to get in the passenger seat. "This thing sure is mighty fancy," he continued to joke as the kids laughed at his accent. "So you can really afford this thing off of taking all those pictures for those high school kids, huh?" The joke turned into a serious question and Elizabeth was caught off guard. Frank could tell that she was caught off guard and tried to come to the rescue. "You're looking really good, even after all these years," he said.

"Oh, put on your seatbelt old man, so I can get these kids to some ice cream," she shot down his advance with a smile.

"Well, yes, mama," Frank said and the kids once again began to laugh.

Elizabeth placed the SUV in reverse, backed out of her parking spot, and almost hit a child speeding along on a bicycle. The car came to a jerking stop as she hit the brakes.

"Never did know how to drive any," Frank said and Elizabeth returned the statement with a sharp smack to his chest. "That hurt," he said as he jumped and began to rub the area Elizabeth's hand had struck.

"Well, you shoulda learned years ago to keep your mouth shut," Elizabeth looked at him with a wide smile as she finished removing the bulky SUV from its parking area. It was all Frank could do to keep himself from chasing after that smile with a kiss. He knew however that that would be the fastest way to ruin what he thought he had a chance at starting again. Everything was going well and he didn't want to mess it up now so he chilled himself and started playing with the radio as Elizabeth navigated the vehicle down the driveway and out onto the small county highway that lead into town.

The kids began to shout out numbers to their favorite stations on the radio and started singing. "These dang kids now a days are smarter than we ever were at such a young age. All these cartoons and stuff really do help," Frank said, more impressed with the kids' remembrance at which stations they liked than trying to make conversation.

"Yeah, well it seems that the cartoons they watch now are more educational than time consuming. They know how to suck the children in and make them pay attention to what they are trying to teach without even letting the children know that they are learning anything. It's crazy, you know? Both those kids can count, know their ABC's, and are potty trained," Elizabeth said as she was intrigued by Frank's observation.

"Well, that's because they have my blood in them. My DNA is perfection," Frank said and Elizabeth jumped on the misstatement.

"Oh? So Steph has your DNA in her, huh, Superman? How did you manage to make that one happen?" Elizabeth poked with another one of her beaming smiles.

"Hey, don't doubt me," Frank exclaimed matching Elizabeth's tone.

The rest of the short drive was filled with laughter and singing from the back seat as the kids rambled the words to every song on the radio. Frank continuously caught himself trying not to stare at Elizabeth as she was driving. Elizabeth continuously caught Frank staring at her, but didn't say anything as she didn't want to shoot the man down or make him feel awkward. She knew Frank and knew that if she called him out, he was likely to either bottle up or get defensive. That was the old him, she thought to herself. I wonder if he's changed that as well. She was glad, after all, that Frank was staring at her like that. It had been a long time since she felt wanted and even if it was with a man who at one time she felt like was lower than the scum of the earth, it felt nice. She began to coach herself in her brain that she would not let him back into her life the way he wanted to waltz right in. She knew he would find a way inside and, if he had really changed, she was ok with that. She just had to make sure the change was real.

"You going to slow down or just Dukes of Hazard it?" Frank's voice yanked Elizabeth from her thoughts as she passed the turn off to the ice cream shop. She was so deep in thought that she had managed to not even be paying attention to where she was going. She made a U-turn, embarrassed, and pulled into the parking lot.

Frank got out of the car first still laughing at Elizabeth. Embarrassed, she got out of the vehicle and they both took a kid by the hand as they walked across the parking lot. A few old ladies sitting in the gazebo drinking coffee began to whisper in a low tone. Elizabeth knew that they were talking about them, but she didn't care. The whole town knew about the break up and by tomorrow the town would know that Frank and Elizabeth had been spotted together again. Frank felt the exact same way and made sure to pause for a second and say, "hi," to them. Elizabeth and the kids continued to walk towards the door.

"You ladies planning on making it out to the complex to watch any games this year?" Frank questioned. He knew it was going to drive them nuts for him to yank them from their whispers about his personal endeavors.

"Maybe when baseball starts. I don't know anything about this soccer riff-raff going on now. I miss the days when football was everything," one of the ladies spoke up.

"Well, I'll be glad to see you there then," Frank said with a wider smile. She knew the lady had said what she said out of spite, as old folks always hated change. He ran to catch up with Elizabeth and the children and caught them in time to open the door to the same place where he had started the new chapter in his life with Heather almost four months ago.

# PART 33

The four of them walked inside the small ice cream shop and to the front counter. The kids ordered the normal medium twist cones and the adults ordered a couple coffees. "I'll pay for it," Frank immediately took out his leather wallet, pulled out a twenty dollar bill, and handed it to the woman.

"Money bags, huh?" Elizabeth said with a smile. She had taken notice that Frank's wallet was a little more plump now than it had been three or four years prior. She wondered in that moment what it would have taken for Frank to make the changes he made if Landon hadn't have died. She saw the exuberance of youth in this late thirties male. It was the same gleam that she had spotted her freshman year of high school. He looked good and was apparently doing well and she was surprised, as she had never taken the time after the divorce to even think twice about Frank.

"Well, since I got the junk yard cleaned up and orderly and the new used lot I threw together . . . . Yeah, things have turned around," Frank said trying to convey that he really had changed more than Elizabeth knew.

The kids rushed to the booth they were familiar with and sat down. They kept each other content as Elizabeth and Frank talked. "So, I mean, what did you have in mind with this ice cream, Frank?" Elizabeth said as she stared intently down at the table. Frank knew that the questions were about to start flying in his direction. If he knew anything about this woman in front of him, he knew her body language. The way she was staring down at the table matched the expression she had shown when she told him she was leaving. He knew that she was running and scared because of what he had done before. She looked back up at him with a smile, "I . . . . I, uh, I'm sorry." Frank stopped the apology in its tracks.

"Don't apologize to me, Elizabeth. And calm that restless mind of yours and let's just enjoy our time with the grandchildren. I simply wanted a chance to get close enough to stare into those gorgeous eyes of yours again, even if for a second. I'm just looking for something that will make everything worth it."

Somehow the compliment made her blush and she felt a little safer. Frank noticed how well she had taken it and his mind began its own happy prance. He wanted to tell her everything about how the last three years of his life had went and how everything had lead up to this point, but he knew when to push it and this just wasn't the time for pushing.

"So, how are the pictures coming?" Frank questioned. Elizabeth had gone to photography school after Landon's death to try to get her mind off of everything. She, like Frank, had become distant to the world and everyone except for her grandchild and Heather. Photography had become her passion and she was surprised Frank was interested.

"Well, you know, it's getting to be about school time again. So I'm pretty booked up for the next three months with senior pictures. I have some weddings, too."

"Well, hell, what did we pay for our wedding pictures? I know it was over a thousand. That's . . . wow, that's impressive, Elizabeth," Frank once again stepped on her toes in the conversation. He couldn't fight his excitement and his mind raced as he thought of their wedding day. "You know that, besides the day Landon was born, was the absolute most wonderful and amazing day I had had in my entire life." Elizabeth was not expecting Frank to follow up the excitement with such a deep statement. She hadn't heard him talk like that since before his father died. The depth and clarity was in his mind that had made her fall in love before.

"Yeah, me, too," she said with a deep sigh in the midst of her thoughts.

"Where did it all go? I mean, not 'where did it all go,' but if I wanted to find it again . . . Do you think? Just never mind," Frank was stumbling over the questions he wanted to ask. He wanted the answers, but was scared to death of them at the same time. It's hard for an old dog to learn any new trick and he knew tricking Elizabeth into falling for him a second time would be harder than the first.

"Frank, I think you said something about just enjoying the night. How about we do that before we get into any deep concerning questions?" Elizabeth tried to comfort Frank.

Frank was put off, but he knew he had stepped over some boundaries he shouldn't have crossed. He felt like kicking himself for trying to erase what six years apart had done to his relationship with Elizabeth. He knew it would be impossible to replace over night the hate with love.

"So you said something about a used car lot?" Elizabeth asked a question to get Frank to break the awkward silence their conversation has sunk into.

"Well, yeah . . . I, uh . . . you know, I'm good with cars, so I've been taking the junk ones that people bring in for scrap and such and restoring them for use. Trying to put that associate's degree to work for me finally. I managed to set up a paint booth last week even." Elizabeth just sat and listened as the man began to ramble. Frank was in love with cars and he always had been. The degree he spoke of was off a scholarship he had won in skills competitions. Either way, she was glad to see it was being put to use and he was following the dreams he had spoken of over a decade ago.

Frank had fallen back into a comfort zone with the question and finished his rambling. He took a sip of his coffee and asked a mind numbing question, "So did you see Heather and Kareen kiss after that high school game?" Elizabeth spit the coffee she was sipping on out and the children were overwhelmed with laughter. "You, uh, saw that too?" Frank questioned again, figuring that her reaction was more over surprise that he had seen.

"Yeah, how could I have not?" She didn't know what to tell Frank and she waited for him to take the conversation further. Heather still confided everything in Elizabeth, so the woman was already aware of the love affair that had been going on.

"I mean what do you think it means? I know that kids these days are changing, but shoot, how do you explain something like that?" Frank began to go further. He was one of the old school types so Elizabeth was not surprised that something like this shocked Frank so much.

She tried to ease his mind, "Well, you know, I figure she just did it out of excitement. You know that girl's life has been rocked in the last, what? About four years now? Nothing for her is the way she pictured it."

"Yeah, I just don't know. I guess you're right. The young girl has had a lot happen to her." He paused and took the final sip of his coffee. "She's doing pretty well for herself, though, between taking over the small store and the house she's living in. I guess even if she and Kareen did become lesbian lovers it wouldn't be anything I couldn't get over. The two do work really well together and these two kids have more than they need. The town on the other hand . . . ." His voice trailed off. He wondered what would happen to everything if the town really found out.

Elizabeth picked up the slack in the conversation, "You know I don't know what's going on between the two of them," Elizabeth lied. "But it's like you said, whatever happens, they are doing well and work together amazingly for these kids. To be honest with you, Frank, this town can go to hell. It doesn't really matter what they think. Besides, we're acting just like them anyways with this speculation." Elizabeth was continuously trying to hide the fact that she knew more than she was letting on.

"Yeah, I guess we will just see," Frank answered.

# PART 34

"We're going to have to be getting them home," Elizabeth said trying to change the conversation.

"Yeah, let's do that," Frank said. He knew that Elizabeth knew more about the situation than she was letting on, but also knew not to press the woman. Both stood up and let the kids out. They ran for the door and together opened it to let the adults out into the cool early autumn air. They walked over to the car and all hopped inside. Elizabeth buckled both children in as to save time from Frank fumbling around.

"So, I'll drop you off at home and then take them home," Elizabeth said. Frank was deflated. In a manner, he was hoping to at least get a few moments alone with Elizabeth, but knew better than to push his luck. The ride was quiet this time because the toddlers had passed out almost instantaneously when the vehicle started moving. After about ten minutes, Frank's driveway came into view and Elizabeth followed it up to his doorstep, not failing to notice the work being done on the century old house.

"So what all you getting done to this old shack?" Elizabeth said as Frank started to get out of the vehicle.

"Well, I tend to have time since I'm my own boss, so I'm fixing it up. Figured I'd get out from underneath some of that crusty money."

"Bout time," Elizabeth joked and then began to place the vehicle in reverse. Frank placed his hand on hers on top of the gear selector.

"Elizabeth, I would like to do this again." he said this time, his voice even more sincere. He had a gleam in his eye that showed he honestly did mean what he was saying. "I've missed you and I don't know in which way you will be willing, but I would like you in my life," He continued and waited for Elizabeth to respond.

"Me, too, Frank," Elizabeth said quietly and then she placed the vehicle in reverse. He watched her back down the drive and out onto the country road wondering whether or not it was too early to try and open back up to Elizabeth. He didn't know she was torn inside as well and, if anything, he had definitely made his intentions clear.

The drive the rest of the way, Elizabeth wished the kids were awake. Nothing, not the radio or counting the lines on the road, would push the day out of her head. She raced around the thought of Frank and wondered if she was truly clear on his intentions. She wondered if he wanted her around for friendship or wanted her to be around to be his lover again. She knew she wouldn't make it easy, but it was hard to control herself around that man. He had always had a way of driving her crazy and that was why it took her so long to go through with the divorce. She knew she would never find anyone like Frank to love her the way she wanted to be loved or anyone she would be even remotely comfortable with like she was with him. She wanted him back in the worst way because she could see that he was a changed man. At least her heart wanted him back; her head was telling a different story of caution. The two were fighting a great debate inside her.

Elizabeth brought the vehicle to a halt in Heather's driveway. Heather stood up from where she was rocking on a swing on that big porch and walked down the driveway to help pull the worn out toddlers from the vehicle. Heather was anxious to see how Elizabeth's night had gone with Frank. Elizabeth had told her in their many phone calls that she was always weak to Frank like Heather was to Landon, so Heather was worried that Frank may be able to convert her in one night. "How was it?" Heather asked as they began to walk up the side walk.

"Well, it was, uh . . . . well, okay," Elizabeth responded.

"That doesn't sound too reassuring, momma. Let's get the kids inside and in bed and we can talk about it." Heather knew she needed more information and that Elizabeth would need to release some of the stress of the night from her brain. Heather held the door open for Elizabeth and they both walked up stairs silently as to not wake the children. They both kissed the children on the forehead as they laid them into their separate beds and then walked downstairs where Kareen was already waiting with three glasses of wine in the living room.

"So how was it, Lizzy?" Kareen asked. Elizabeth laughed and grabbed a glass of the wine.

"I didn't even get a, "hi, how you doing," from either one of you. What makes you think a girl can't hold her own?" Elizabeth joked.

"Well, we just know how you felt about this guy. I mean, how often do you and I talk about how much Frank and Landon were so much alike?" Heather questioned. "If they are that much alike, then I know what it's like to be up against them. Remember, I've been there," Heather continued her explanation.

"Yeah, yeah. I definitely know that one, Heather. I watched you. You worshipped the ground Landon walked on," Elizabeth said.

"It was really that bad?" Kareen said in a surprised tone of voice.

"Yeah, it really was. He was everything that made the world go round to me, babe," Heather answered. Even though Elizabeth knew what was going on between the two women it still caught her off guard to hear Heather refer to Kareen as babe.

"Yeah, well enough about me. I want to hear how your night went, Lizzy," Heather interjected turning the spotlight from her painful past.

"Well, I guess I owe you two an explanation," Elizabeth began and both Heather and Kareen nodded for her to continue as they sipped on their wine. She took a drink of her own and continued the story. "He really does seem to be different, guys. I mean, look at everything he's done in the last five months. I know you guys had to prod him to start the fields, but now that he's started that he seems to be starting everything. He has a car lot now and he's working on that old shack of a house we had together and I almost wanted to stop and check it out, you know, linger for a moment longer there, but the kids saved me from myself and doing that. You have no idea how long it had been since I was able to see that clear look in his eyes. I just, I feel like he had so much control over me." She paused to catch her breath to keep herself from rambling, took another sip of her wine and began again.

"You know he's everything I damn wanted," Elizabeth then paused again. She didn't want to let herself fall apart, but the idea of this was shaking her. "I just hate that in one night, over some damn ice cream, he can make me want to just throw my arms around him. His beautiful face is back without all that hair and I just wanted to rest my hand on his cheek and give him a deep kiss before I pulled away . . . . but no . . . I can't let him in that easy." She took another drink of her wine and tried to let the last sentence sink in as if it was an order directly to her own heart.

"Well, I mean, you can't control what your heart wants, Lizzy. But be careful letting him in that quick. You know how dangerous that can be, whether he has changed or not." Heather offered some encouragement in the older woman's direction. They all three took another sip of wine in unison and Kareen filled both glasses.

"Any more of these and I'm probably going to be camping out on your couch," Elizabeth said with a small laugh trying to lighten the situation.

"You know you're welcome anytime. Just drink all you want. You deserve it," Kareen said with a smile.

"Oh yeah, before I forget, Frank asked about you guys," Elizabeth proclaimed.

"Asked about *us*?" Heather instantly questioned.

"Yeah. About the kiss," Elizabeth continued. The room went silent.

# PART 35

"But, no one saw us . . . ." Heather said in an almost silent tone. She was shocked to hear it even brought up.

"What did you tell him?" Kareen said in an even more defensive tone. The three stared at each other for what seemed an eternity.

"Well, I mean, I didn't tell him anything. I just supported the idea that you guys are doing fine and work as a good team for your children. Frank agreed, too. So, what I'm thinking is: what is making you guys keep this thing a secret? It will have to come out sometime if this is the path you're going to take for the rest of your life." She paused to let her words of advice sink in on the two young females in front of her.

"I'm going to sleep. We can talk more about it tomorrow," Heather broke the silence. The young girl had grown to be hard up, but in rare instances things would still come up that would make her back down. This was one of them.

\* \* \*

"But, what will everyone in the town say? We have our kids, our store . . . just everything." Heather was pacing around the bedroom talking to Kareen. She had also followed Heather upstairs, leaving Elizabeth alone with her thoughts on the couch.

"She's right, Heather. We have to be more open about it. If we expect it to be normal for this town, we need to make it normal for ourselves first and the only way to do that is to get them used to it," Kareen finished and once again the girl was right in Heather's eyes. She just didn't know where to go and what to do. "We don't have to tell anyone anything, babe. Just act closer out in public," Kareen continued her explanation.

"Yeah, I guess you're right. We can start tomorrow. You know it's our afternoon to work at the store," Heather responded. Kareen pulled Heather to the bed and gave her a kiss on the forehead.

"Rest that pretty little head of yours. Tomorrow's another day," Kareen said and Heather obliged, laying her head back on the pillow. She felt Kareen's arm drape around her as she wondered off to sleep inside a mixture of rapid thoughts.

* * *

The next day, when the girls awoke, they walked downstairs to find that Elizabeth was already gone and her blanket was folded on the couch. The kids were not awake yet, so they decided to share a cup of coffee. "So, I mean, I don't know about this whole going public thing," Heather broke the initial silence. "I don't know about, you know, just airing out our personal life to the whole town." Kareen stared at Heather for a few moments before deciding to break the silence.

"I don't understand where you think we are airing our personal business to the public or how we have to do anything at all today. All Elizabeth was trying to say, is that it's not healthy to hide. If people ask, then we tell them. We aren't putting a damn billboard up in front of the store or anything that says, '"hey, a lesbian couple inside."' Heather sipped her coffee almost embarrassed by how she had reacted. She, once again, like every time before, knew that Kareen was right.

"Mommy," Heather heard Braylen call from upstairs and she went to grab her child. He always called out for he when he reached the steps so he would know whether she was downstairs or in her room. Rather smart for a child his age. She walked upstairs and bathed each child separately, getting them ready for the day. They were going to go to Heather's parents like normal when the girls worked at the store. "Grandpa Frank is funny," Braylen said as Heather was washing his golden orange hair. Heather was surprised at how warm and comforting it felt inside her to hear her child speak of both grandparents in the same tone. Six months ago she would have never thought that Braylen would grow to know his grandfather, much less love him. She began to recount in her head the last almost four years of her child's life and how everything had drastically changed from the beginning of everything until now. From birth up until now, nothing had been simple. She let her mind wander while drying the child.

It was all a blur in her head, really, from the death of Landon, to first holding Braylen, then to the first time meeting Kareen. She laughed out loud as she began to recount in her mind how she had been so standoffish to her now partner. "Times will change everything," she whispered and the child gave her a confused look. Heather smiled at the cute face she was receiving from the child. Her thoughts continued further from the first real conversation she had had with Kareen at that memorial for Landon until the first night she spent with the woman and, that at the time, awkward kiss they shared. Who would have known that three years later they would have such a bond? Furthermore, who would have known that Frank and Elizabeth would be talking at all? "Landon would have been so glad to see his parents talking," Heather once again let a whisper stray out of her mouth.

"Daddy?" Braylen replied. Braylen was reminded constantly who his father was and at times questioned where his father was. It struck something inside Heather to hear Braylen say that one word and a single tear trailed down her face. It still crushed her that Braylen would never know his father. It somehow made all her problems seem tiny in the grand scheme of things.

"You okay?" Kareen said as she noticed the tear streaming down Heather's cheek. She had walked upstairs unnoticed to help out with the children.

"Yeah, I was just thinking about the past and how Landon would have taken everything. I did what I always do and let words slip out of my mouth." Kareen smiled as she knew exactly what Heather was talking about. "Well, I let Landon's name slip out of my mouth and Braylen automatically recognized the name and whispered, 'daddy,' back to me.... It's just, you know, good to hear him say Landon's name and recognize that that is his father." Kareen let go off Steph's hand and walked over to Heather. Kareen wiped the tear off her face before placing her hands around the woman waist.

"Yeah, I understand what you're saying, babe, but please smile for me. The past is the past and there isn't a thing we can do about it. Nothing will bring him back and nothing will bring Jason back. We only have each other now and that's the best we can wish for." Kareen followed it with another one of her comforting kisses on the forehead.

"I know, I know .... It's just good that he knows, too," Heather answered looking down at Braylen. "Let's finish getting you dressed," she said forcing a smile on her face.

*   *   *

The day went as planned. They took over at the shop at noon and closed it at ten. Heather and Kareen had not worked at the store more than an hour at a time since soccer season started and were surprised to see how far the teenagers had carried it. All the books were spot on and were accounted for by Lisa nightly. Business was busier than what they were used to when the store opened up, but that again would explain why they had to order everything at a faster rate lately. They also had to stay open a half an hour later as the dining room, or at least the four booths set up, had still been full at closing time. The duo began cleaning everything around the four tables and reiterated to the elderly couples not to worry about leaving in a hurry. Heather was singing to herself lightly wondering how in the world they were supposed to let it out to the public about her and Kareen. Amidst the thoughts and sweeping she didn't notice Kareen walking up behind her. Kareen placed her hands around Heather's waist and gave her a small kiss on the lips in full view of the booths.

"That should give them some type of idea," Kareen said answering Heather's thoughts. Looking at the tables, Heather could tell Kareen was right, as the ladies were already whispering and their eyes jerked away in her view. Now what madness will this bring, she thought as she stared down at the floor, feeling every stare as it burned through her.

# PART 36

The ladies eating stood up, emptied their trays, and walked hurriedly to the door. "Thanks for the food. It was delicious as always," one managed to say as she walked through. Heather somehow felt a sense of embarrassment over what had happened, but she knew not to question Kareen's logic. Kareen had came out on top so many times before that it was probably illogical to try and find the source of explanation for the kiss.

"How much longer you think you will be?" Kareen broke Heather out of her silence "I think we should tell your parents what happened before it gets around town too much. And you know that Thelma Mae will be telling everyone in church. We're big sinners now, you know?" Kareen had a menacing smile spread wide across her face.

"What do you mean tell my parents, Kareen? I thought we weren't going to broadcast this to the whole town." Heather was up in an uncommonly defensive tone. She didn't like the idea and she knew it would be trouble when her parents found out.

"Don't worry, babe. I'm your anchorwoman and I'll tell the whole story," Kareen said, failing to calm Heather down.

Heather figured she would let Kareen do exactly what she wished and tell the whole world if she wanted. They then hopped in the car and headed to Heather's parents house. Heather felt her stomach sink as the driveway came into view. She wanted to say something, anything, to try to make Kareen change her mind, but she knew it would be no use. When Kareen was set on something, she usually did it one way or another. Heather just found herself once again wishing she would have been granted some sort of warning before that kiss.

"Well, let's do this," Kareen said as she hopped bouncily out of the car. Heather forced a smile and followed her partner inside. Heather could see her mother and father were in a good mood and the kids were asleep. She waited as small talk was made for Kareen to push the subject out into full view. She didn't have to wait long and she heard the words release from Kareen's mouth. "You guys, we sort of have something to talk about," Kareen offered the beginning of the conversation as if it was a joke. The rest became a blur to Heather.

Heather was actually pleasantly surprised at her parent's reaction. "Well, I mean we sort of figured," Dan began. "You guys have been living together now for what, almost four years, and neither of you have been out on a date. Your mother and I both witnessed that kiss and, well, we don't like it, but our grandchild is taken care of and you're happy, so what can we really do?" Dan ended his initial reaction and Heather was pulled out the blur that she thrust herself into.

"Your father's right, Heather. We support you guys without supporting you guys, if that makes any damn sense at all?" Oh, no, Heather thought to herself, here goes my mother cursing again. This can't be good. "Just don't go all 'MTV Real World' on us and start yelling it to the public," Lisa finished with a small laugh as she was trying to lighten the conversation.

"Thank you," Heather said and a small tear streamed down her face as she hugged both her parents. Kareen remained where she was sitting with a small gratified smile. She, too, was surprised at Dan and Lisa's reaction, but she didn't plan on showing it.

\* \* \*

The following day, the children had practice. Frank was nowhere to be found at the start of practice, so Dan began running the kids through the normal warm up routines. Fifteen minutes into practice, Elizabeth's vehicle sped up the drive and Frank hopped out next to the field. Laughter was spread between Frank and Elizabeth and to anyone a sense of love was visible.

"Oh, no," Kareen exclaimed. "I have a good feeling where she disappeared to a couple nights ago when we asked her to stay." Heather began to answer, but Kareen had already risen off her spot on the bleachers and began jogging to Elizabeth's car. Heather walked up and caught the two in mid conversation. Apparently, Kareen had already started grilling Elizabeth.

"What do you expect? I mean I was lonely and I never really stopped loving him. I really think we can make things work this time."

"Well, okay. Just don't get yourself hurt, Elizabeth," Kareen's motherly tactics were kicking in on the much older woman. "Better yet, how about you and Frank take a walk around town with me and Heather after practice?" Elizabeth agreed and Heather already knew where this was going to go.

After practice, the girls dropped the kids off at Heather's and met Frank and Elizabeth at the coffee shop, interrupting a kiss as they pulled up. Frank had an even larger glow on his face than he had been carrying.

"Well, let's go," Frank said and handed the girls coffees that had already been waiting on them. "I remembered what you ordered, so I just ordered Kareen the same thing. I figured you probably had the same tastes, seeing as how you're lovers and all." Lisa punched Frank in the stomach and the conversation grew awkwardly quiet. Frank sensed his mistake and tried to fix the issue. "Now I didn't mean it in a bad way. That kiss in the store last night is already the talk around town and I . . . . I was just joking." Kareen was agitated and decided to break the mood of the joke.

"What you mean this," she questioned and before Heather could respond she felt herself being yanked in Kareen's direction. She didn't fight it; she simply kissed Kareen back and smiled as they both turned back in Frank's direction. "You mean that?" Kareen offered.

Frank was too stunned to say too much of anything. The three women laughed as he struggled to find a way to close his jaw that had dropped seemingly mere inches from the ground at viewing the kiss. "Well, we were going to tell you politely, Frank, on this walk, but you know you just had to open your mouth," Kareen once again found a way to break the silence.

"Yeah, I mean . . . . uh, that does it. You confirmed the word," Frank said nervously and the four of them this time broke into laughter. They began walking down Main Street and stopped inside their own store to get a bite to eat. Heather couldn't help but think about how things used to be. She stared out the window and thought of the thousands of times she would stop at this same little store to talk to Landon as he was pumping gas. His memories were still haunting her after all this time.

"What about you guys? You know you're the talk of town, too, and the way you pulled up to the soccer field late today, Frank. That's answering a few questions yourself."

"What can I say?" Frank laughed. "I wanted something and I went after it and she came crawling back . . . half drunk, but she made it." Heather zoned out of the rest of the conversation. She once again felt like everything was going back to normal. Normal from what, she had no clue because nothing in her life was any sort of normal.

The years began to fly by in a blur for Heather. The week after that walk had been filled to the brim with slander and gossip, but the girls were able to make it through all the wreckage that was their love life, unscathed. A small town is a brutal place to be the center of attention at, but thankfully the town also took into account the life that the females had made for themselves and other families with the store and the complex.

The fact that the women were able to become partners in the town's eyes without becoming outcasts was a testament to how much they had really done for that small community. The elderly people still whispered, even now, a year after, but that is simply what old people do. The females had no clue how fast life would fly by now that they had found a sense of normalcy, but the years clicked by without warning.

* * *

Heather was awoken by a rustling in the kitchen and the smell of blueberry pop tarts. "What's going on?" she called downstairs waiting to hear a squeaky answer from her son's now changing voice. She stood up and stared face to face at a woman in her early thirties. "Where the hell did time go?" She pleaded with the mirror to somehow change the time back to those days when the kids were smaller.

"It seems like a dream, doesn't it?" Heather looked as if she would burst into tears at any moment so Kareen stood up to comfort her mate of going on eleven years now.

"Well, hun, I know it seems like our lives were just beginning yesterday, but we have to face it. It's the first day of Middle School and we have to let our little Prep and Jock out into this big world sometime. It will be okay, girl. The four of us will always be okay no matter what comes our way and you know that." Kareen gave Heather a small kiss on the cheek.

"I know," she paused again. "I really know . . . . I just wish I would have listened to my mother and savored the time more. I knew it would go fast, but damn. I swear just yesterday I was changing diapers." The conversation was broken by a kid who had just hit twelve. Braylen was now becoming a tall and lean red-headed replica of his father. His looks reminded Heather daily of the past.

"Let's go, mom. I was late for the first day of sixth grade. I won't be late my first day of seventh grade, too. Remember, I have a game tonight," Braylen began barking orders and Heather threw on some clothes, rushing out of the house to the kids already waiting in the car.

# PART 37

Braylen was right. He had a game that night. Heather had completely forgotten.

"Love you, mom. Don't forget." Both kids jumped out of the car and walked briskly up to the large building that Heather had once called her own. She couldn't believe that the years flew by at the rate they had. She rubbed the rest of the sleep out of her eyes and began to drive to the store where Kareen was supposed to meet her. The town had not aged in all those years because it's not possible for an old town to get any older than it already was. The small town was a painted picture that never changed and Heather viewed everything now just as she had as a child. The kids running for the bus and the elderly taking laps around town with a smile. Everything was just as she had always remembered. She pulled into the store, pleasantly surprised at the rate at which the addition had been going on.

"Well, what do you think?" Kareen said as she was sitting on the front step and could already read Heather's expression.

"I really, really think it's going to be good. This little place needed a bigger restaurant from the day we took it over, anyways.

"Yeah, we got a long day ahead of us you know. You over that crying you were doing this morning?" Kareen joked.

"Yeah, I'm not going to be over that crying until we're on that long winding road to Braylen's game. I hate going clear over to Meadowsville for away games."

"Cry baby, cry baby, cry baby . . ." Kareen interrupted Heather and then hugged her. Heather pushed her away.

"I'm not a damn crybaby. I just hate the fact that it seems like every day I wake up, a thousand more years have gone by. I hate when my mother is right and in this situation she definitely was. I just want everything to slow down. I'm not crying." Kareen attempted to wrap her arms around Heather but Heather pushed her away and the two laughed as they walked inside.

They day crept by as Heather dreaded the long ride to the game that night. She found that everything she had rolled her eyes at as a teenager affected her now. The simplest things could throw her mood into disarray and the rest of the day would just be flushed down the toilet bowl laughing as it circled around and around. "Getting old sucks," she yelled back to Kareen as she was getting things ready to switch shifts with the high school teens.

"Heather, we are in our early thirties. That is by no means old," Kareen said with a smile "What has it been with you today, whiney ass?" she continued to joke. Even after a decade of being together Kareen was still able to make Heather feel like she was protected and that she was stressing the small things more than she really needed to. It was nothing like she had pictured her future almost thirteen years ago, but she knew that she wouldn't take it back. The thoughts of Landon were memories of the time they spent together and not of the horror of his death. Everything about her life was worked out.

Frank and Elizabeth met Heather and Kareen outside at just past three to ride to the game together. Frank and Elizabeth had got remarried and were still cherishing that puppy love they somehow kept into their early fifties now. Frank had managed to turn that shack into a very nice modern house and the used car lot now held over twenty cars at all times. The junk yard behind the house in the field had been completely removed now. The soccer complex was still going strong after ten years of use. Another game field had been created and the football team had a practice field there. Frank was still happy to run it all in his spare time and was actually known for giving back to the community, instead of the drunken worthless father. Not often does a town change a broken image for someone, but the four individuals now sitting in that SUV had all changed what that town thought was normal. Heather and Kareen were not thought of as a lesbian couple, in a sense, but just really good friends. Everybody knew, but it was brushed out of view, just as Frank's drinking problem had been. Another testament of how times really can change, if not, the appearance, but the mentality of a small town.

Heather whined and complained the entire ride to Braylen's game as the rest of the car poked fun at her the whole way. They pulled up to the opposing team's field and found Lisa, Dan, and Steph already waiting.

"Well, this one's going to be a good one," Dan said as Frank walked up. The two shook hands and walked to the sideline. "That goalie is years above the rest of the team. We're really going to have to catch him back door if we want to score. I hope that coach knows that and let's the kids know to take advantage of the crosses." Frank wasn't surprised to see that Dan was already able to give a full scouting report. Dan always arrived at every game early to watch the teams warm up. It had been a few years since the pair coached the kids, but they both still had that coach mentality.

"How's Braylen looking?" Frank questioned, knowing he was about to get that scouting report as well.

"Well, for twelve, you know, he's hitting the back of the net twenty five yards out and apparently he has his daddy's head. I'm guessing he will get one in today off a header. That's probably the only way to catch that goalie sleeping."

The game started with Braylen playing at a center mid-field. Mid-field for soccer is known as one of the most well rounded positions as you're expected to have the stamina and ball control and straight up physical presence to be able to play offense just as fast as defense. Braylen harnessed all those skills. He was tall enough to knock the opposition off of the ball, but also fast enough to make the runs streaking up and down the field required by a mid-fielder. The first half flew by without a goal. Both teams had managed to put shots on goal, but nothing was misdirected or well placed enough in the corners to really knock either goalie off guard. After the whistle blew for half time, Braylen ran over to the sidelines to get his drink from his mother.

"Braylen, you have to catch him with misdirection. Have them send some crosses in and get a head on it. Sure enough, one will go in," Dan offered some advice before the early teen ran back onto the field.

"Gotcha, pop pop," Braylen said before he ran to join his team.

"Goooaaaaaalllll!" A low murmur came from the home team's crowd. The opposing team had sent a cross in about five minutes into the second half and it bounced off of one of Braylen's teammates into their own goal. You could see the air deflated out of the team.

"That will probably be all we see in this one," Frank said as the smile disappeared from his face.

"Yeah . . . ." Dan said, equally down as the team out on the field. Ten minutes passed and the team started to get their legs back underneath them. Passes were starting to string together as they bounded down the sideline. Braylen received a ball at midfield and carried to the eighteen, dribbling around two players along the way. He then passed the ball off to the left wing, who carried it to the corner. The wing then placed the ball lofting just over the turned goalies head. The ball was out in front of Braylen and the kid slid to get a leg on it. The ball hit laces and glanced off his boot kissing off the post before it rested into the back of the net. "Goooaaaaaalllll!" Dan screamed. His advice had worked and they were back to dead even.

Ten minutes were left in the game and it was clear which team now had the momentum. The home team had carried the lead off the lucky goal for thirty minutes to see it yanked back to even with that almost textbook play. "This team is going to take state in four years," Dan predicted as the sidelines calmed after the goal. It was still foreign for Heather and the ladies beside her to watch two die hard football fans turn to support this sport as well.

"Yeah, probably with some luck," Frank replied and turned back to watching the game. The game winded down, back and forth, to three minutes as both teams began to get anxious for something to give. The game evolved away from the technical skill put on display earlier to more of a sense of a play ground game. Both teams were out of energy and were simply coasting to a tie. Braylen had the ball at his feet at midfield and was settling for what appeared to be mere ball control. One seemingly bad touch and the ball bounced to the side of Braylen and he placed laces on the ball giving it lift. The ball soared from about thirty yards out and hit the square crossbar. The ball then bounced off the back of the goalie and rolled slowly into the net. Braylen fell to his knees and the team pulled him back to his feet.

"Wow! That was lucky," Dan exclaimed in Frank's direction.

"Hey, sometimes luck is all you need," Frank replied. The game ended two to one, ending with an undefeated season at 20-0-02, the first in county history for any sports team.

# PART 38

As the years rushed by, time kept its pace. It was a rush between school, soccer, volleyball, and the restaurant. Heather could barely find time to keep up with all the madness that was pushed on her plate from day to day. The kids were older now and hitting stages in their lives that she had felt like she lived just days ago. She tried to clutch on to every moment as she knew that it was going to swirl away from her as easily as paper in a light breeze. Braylen had turned into his own free spirit, but that free spirit was hiding a secret. In his adolescence, he had fallen for a girl. Steph was his sister, without being his sister, and Braylen could not help but give in to the attraction for this dark haired girl that had a body just like her mothers. Steph had grown to be a replica of her mother, and was raised beside Braylen. Under any other circumstance, Braylen could just walk up to her and use his athletic appearance and his inviting smile to win her over, but she was his sister and something like that could destroy their relationship.

Most of Braylen's freshman year had been about trying to just keep up. He had easily made the varsity squad in soccer and they managed to have a decent season as they won more than they lost. He had fifteen goals that year, which is pretty outstanding for a freshman, but as every adolescent teen does, he began to search for more. He carried the secret inside him and the feelings churned every morning. Every morning, Steph would ask Braylen, "How do I look?" and give the same model twirl. He wanted to give her a small kiss, or something, to let her know how she really looked, but only managed to tell her she was beautiful. He knew it would either go drastically right and then they would have a secret just like their parents had had before, or on the flip side, it could go drastically wrong and everything he worked for could be ruined. He decided to keep the secret inside of him until he felt like everything was safe. Someday, he knew he would have to tell, but not today, and more than likely, not even this year.

He managed his first two years of high school to find a sense of popularity. He was good at a sport, physically attractive, and his parents had money to buy him the nice clothes, so he automatically fit in. He was doing well academically and scored more goals in soccer his sophomore year than his freshman year, but wasn't completely outstanding to anyone in that town. The elderly still whispered about how it was such a sad story that the boy was not playing football as his daddy had done and Braylen almost felt cursed by that. How could they judge him off of what his father had done sixteen years ago? He didn't even know his father and hated him for the fact that he perished from this world leaving him nothing but a legacy to carry on. He managed to carry it, however, and twist it in the direction he wanted it to go. If he wanted to do something he was going to do it and probably twice as fast because he didn't feel he should conform to any damn legacy. He wasn't his father, but decided to ask his mother about it to try and find out who his father was. He felt he needed to get over the sense of hate that everything in the last couple years had brought him.

"Who was Landon?" he asked his mother over breakfast. Heather was shocked. She had only heard Braylen speak of Landon a couple of times and then he had called Landon by dad or daddy.

"What do you mean? What do you want to know, babe?" Heather prodded for more information from her son.

"I don't know. I just have to know about him. Everybody asks me all the time why I'm not playing football or why I'm doing this or that. I feel like everybody expects me to just be him all over again and I hate him for that. All he did for me was leave some damn legacy. Am I supposed to just pick up where he left off?" Heather could see the frustration in her son's face and his voice. Her mind went back to the times when she laid on her bed and cried because she knew what the future would hold without Landon. She just wished he was here so that this discussion wouldn't be needed.

"I knew this would happen," she began in her soft motherly tone trying to calm her son. "I knew while I was still pregnant with you that you would have to grow up in his footsteps. See, I know you know what your dad was about because of all the newspaper articles that compare you to him every time you do something good, but you really don't know him. Your father was a down to earth guy that had everything ripped from him the moment he felt he had the whole world. I just wish you would have been able to meet him."

"Well, I definitely can't do that. I guess I don't care. I just, I don't know, it doesn't solve anything," Braylen cut off his mother's rambling. "I just want to be my own person."

Heather found herself saying a small prayer for her son as he got up from the table and walked away. She knew that he simply wanted to fit in and couldn't blame him for being bitter. She didn't know, however, how twisted the kid's life would be growing up without a father. Dealing with the town thinking he was a letdown, even though he was near perfection at the sport he played. Finally and most of all trying to hide the love he had for a female so very close to him yet so far away. Braylen carried a lot on his shoulders for such a young age, but until now Heather had no indication that it had bothered him. He jogged up the steps and began to get ready for practice.

His junior year met him with more expectations. Even in the scouting reports his team was predicted to make an appearance at the state tournament. It would be the first time in school history that any sport besides football had won any title and Braylen was confident this would be the year people would actually start to respect his sport. He also knew that it would give him a chance to fill that legacy that he hated and the thing that tortured him the most was that no matter how much he hated it, he wanted to live up to what his father was.

The season went well, and the team won even more games than the year before. Braylen was noticed by larger colleges that were known for their soccer programs and was beginning to receive notices and letters daily inquiring about the boy's dreams and where he wanted to go with his soccer career. He began to be lifted into the place he had always dreamed he would be. The fact that the team had managed to score more points that year than the beloved football team also played a huge role with cementing the soccer limelight into the town. It took over a decade, but the town was starting to support, instead of recognize, the soccer team and turnouts at the games began to rise. The complex made more money off these larger turn outs and made everything nicer. New scoreboards for all fields and paved parking lots were just a few of the editions that Frank and Dan had managed to add to the Landon Maston Memorable Complex.

The team fell short of the state championship title they were predicted to bring home, but was only to lose two seniors to graduation. Braylen knew that they stood a better chance of winning the state championship the following year, anyways, so throughout his junior year he maintained a level of intensity with the sport. The top eleven on the team bonded like a family and traveled the east coast on the weekends entering into indoor tournaments. All of them knew that if there was going to be a year that they did anything worth remembering it would have to be this year. Braylen used that to try and push away the thoughts he had of Steph in his mind, but she was still there. Literally, she was still there. If she wasn't at her volleyball matches or busy with something else, she attended every soccer match to watch her Landon. A secret love had brewed in both directions but bôth held it inside only wondering what it could bring for them. Their junior year flew by, leaving only one more stab at greatness for Braylen and, with any luck, an impossible couple. Not so impossible by today's standards, however. When taking a glance at their parents, anything could happen.

# PART 39

The team had managed to consistently place in the larger east coast tournaments throughout the off season and was gaining a national spotlight for Braylen's senior season. The amount of time he had put in the sport, from the early age of three until now at almost eighteen, had proven to be worth something. Even through the bitter loss at the state championship, Braylen was still receiving a lot of college inquiries. He was looking more towards a place that had the small town country atmosphere and was looking to sign with West Virginia University in Morgantown, West Virginia. The Mountaineers consistently had a team ranked in the top ten of the NCAA and Braylen felt that if he could do well, he could gain a chance to play professionally as well. That would be an end state of fulfilling the legacy that his father left behind and give that small town a reason to remember him, besides the fact that he was Landon Maston's son. First, though, he had this year in front of him.

The soccer team worked hard for their senior season knowing that if any one of them were to be remembered, then it would have to be this year. This year, the state tournament was to be held at their own home field at Landon Maston Memorable Complex. The school had placed the bid and, after inspection, the state board was impressed with the complex and unanimously passed for Christian County to be the place of the tournament. There was a small buzz in the town throughout the season, as the team picked up wins, as to what it would mean if soccer took state. Braylen had been moved to play left striker for his senior year as the coach wanted to use Braylen's natural left foot dominance and speed to catch the opposing teams off guard. Everyone knew who Landon was, however, because of the national spotlight his team had received at tournaments in the off season. He could score on the national level, which made scoring on a small country region, cake work. None of it would mean anything to anyone, though, if he was not able to bring the state title back to that town. He would still be a disappointment to everyone if he was not able to carry with his team a trophy into the cabinets of his school that were already weighted with football accomplishments.

So the team worked hard, putting in extra time after every practice to make sure that no one was let down. The work paid off, too, as they began the season crushing nearly every opponent that they came across in that town. The soccer team was able to outscore the football team even with the six point scoring difference. The team had become a family and had given that small town something to look forward to. They were all known from the weekly coverage in the county paper which almost always frequented Braylen, his striker counterpart, and the goalie. Even now though, the papers still compared Braylen to his father and Braylen knew it was something he would just have to grow comfortable with. The state tournament was three weeks away and he knew that if it had happened all along then it wasn't going to stop. All he could do was try to outweigh the accomplishments of his father and do something that had never been done before and transform that small town from everything that it knew. He still had a secret beyond sports, however.

Braylen was not able to shake the feelings he had for Steph and grew more attracted to her day by day as she grew more into a woman. She, too, had planned to go to become a Mountaineer off academic scholarships and the bank of mom. She wanted to follow Braylen anywhere he went and although she preferred getting out of hick town, she figured she could settle for couch burning, which is a national past time of the West Virginia college, instead. She knew that Braylen picked the college for its sports program, but it was also widely known for its listing on the top ten party schools in America as well. She knew that girls would be gunning for him at the parties. If she couldn't be the one he was with, then she wanted to be able to have a say in who the lucky lady was. For now though, she would work on cheering her hero to the state tournament for his senior season. Then, maybe in college, she could share her secret admiration to Braylen and nobody would know their lifelong connection.

Steph and Braylen had been made oblivious of the true connection between their fathers on purpose. Kareen and Heather agreed that it was best kept a secret and would deal with it when the time came. Mysteriously, Steph never became curious about her father or at least she never asked questions. Things were still going well for Heather and Kareen and the addition to the store went nicely as well and served now as a meeting place for kids during lunchtime and after school. It was a good change of pace for Heather and Kareen to see kids hanging out there as much as the adults. Frank and Elizabeth had remarried and were living quietly in the house Frank fixed up. Frank was still year round adamant about keeping the complex up to his own heightened standards in the memory of his only and fallen son. He was elated to know that the tournaments would be held in his back yard that year. He and Dan had become good friends and diehard soccer fans, and spent every Sunday afternoon renting out the high school gym for kids to practice their skills in the much faster paced indoor soccer.

A week before the state tournament, after one of the Sunday indoor sessions, Braylen met with his team, the media, and representatives from West Virginia Universtiy at his mother's store. He had broken into the top twenty five of the recruitment class for freshman athletes in college. He had met with college representatives throughout his sophomore year and decided to follow through with his decision to join the Mountaineers. He signed his national letter of intent while Steph sat on his left and Heather on his right. The newspapers took pictures of the hometown hero and everything became a time machine that took Heather back and she could not help but think of eighteen years ago when she was sitting beside Landon as he was signing his letter of intent for college. In the midst of the pictures and the handshakes, Steph clutched onto Braylen's side and getting lost in the emotion and blur of everything managed to grab Braylen's hand. She loved how her hand fit into his like a glove and moments went by before Braylen fed her an awkward glance. She looked up into his dreamy eyes and then realizing his expression was not one of welcome, she jerked her hand away.

"Sorry. I just got wrapped up in the excitement," she said in a nervous voice and then gave him an awkward hug to try to push the moment out of memory, not knowing what Braylen really felt about her hand in his.

He spent the final week up to the state tournament working hard at practice, but his body was going through the motions as his brain played monkey in the middle with reality. Braylen wondered what that moment had meant to Steph and what she meant by putting her hand in his. He hated that he reacted the way he did and wished he would have just pulled her closer. That way he wouldn't have so many questions swirling around in his head. Did she want him as her partner the way he had dreamed or was it a simple gesture of being friendly and showing him that she was by his side throughout the whole thing? He wanted to believe that it was out of friendship because of the fact that it would keep things normal between them, but the one thing about it all that caught him off guard was the fact that she jumped back as soon as she saw the look on his face. He felt that if it was a gesture out of friendship that she would have just told him so and not reacted the way she had.

Their first three games at state were predicted to be easy, but the quarter, semi, and final were going to be tough, so Braylen tried to push Steph out of his mind and focus on the task at hand. A task easier said than done, but with practicing his whole life, Braylen wasn't worried about the final week, anyways. All that truly mattered right now was winning that state championship and maybe, just maybe, Steph would be his bonus. Maybe she could be the one that he spent the rest of his life with; at least, it was all he could hope for moving to college with the woman of his dreams on his side. He knew that everything would become easier in life with her by his side and it tortured his brain wondering what the future held. Days passed ever so slowly that week and Braylen was playing sloppy in practices, but finally the day came the day he could start the transition of making his dreams reality and put all the legacies behind him. None of it would matter out on that field.

Opening day of the state tournament and it was bigger than the previous year. As it had in that small town, soccer had begun to take root all over the nation. Large swarms of media were present and Braylen spent the first two days speaking to reporters about his future plans and where he wanted to go. Steph simply admired him along with her parents and the grandparents from the sidelines, all of them equally excited at what they were watching take place in their own back yard with their own hero. The complex and tournament had also been granted national attention as four of the nation's top twenty five players were going to be making appearances and trying to steal the hardware for their own respective schools. Two of them, Braylen and his counterpart on the right side, were on the home team and the other two were on opposing teams. The Christian County team moved through the first three games as predicted, easily outgunning the sloppy teams with precision passes, creating space, and the textbook plays. Braylen felt fresh and brand new as if he had been reborn into a world where he was king. It was a feeling his father had taken hold of for only eighteen years and Braylen began to slowly understand why his father was such a legacy. He was king in a small town; a king with only three more wars to fight before he would be granted his crown and shed the cape of a legacy.

# PART 40

Braylen woke up on the day of the State Championship game more nervous about anything than he had been his entire life. It would be his final test before he had to step up to a new level of playing. He knew he could do it, but still couldn't fight back the jitters. The previous two games had gone well for the Christian County team. They had won the first game with a two to zero score off of two technically sound plays. The second victory came off of a penalty kick shoot out where there goalie had come up big, making the initial three stops to lift Braylen's team ahead. Those three stops were enough to seal the deal for the small county player to join Braylen at the West Virginia College where he was going to continue his career. Those games were in the past, though, and he had today riding in front of him. Within the next sixteen hours, history would be either made in or against Braylen's favor. It was the longest wait of his life and he found himself unable to eat anything for breakfast before he headed to the field.

He rode over to the field early with Steph and was stunned to see that the turnout had almost doubled from the previous games and there were still hours left before the game. The media had made a spectacle of everything and college representatives from the surrounding states had shown up to look for last minute signees to fill their rosters. Braylen was stopped by a couple of reporters as he began to walk towards the locker room which was established only that year.

"Braylen, you have had nine goals in your five games in this tournament. That's a state record. How are you predicting today's game will go?" a reporter hurriedly grilled him with a question as he shoved a microphone and camera into Braylen's face.

"I mean, obviously, I feel like we are going to win. We have to win. It's my destiny and a legacy I carry for this small town." The reporter was satisfied with the answer, but there was no way for the stranger to truly understand what the small town star had meant.

Braylen was able to pull away from the mob and reunited with Steph for some last minute words before he went into the locker room to get dressed. They stood outside the locker room for a few moments just a few inches apart.

"I can tell you're nervous," she said as she nervously glanced into his eyes.

"Yeah, it's just . . . you know, I have to win today. I have to do well or I will let the whole town down." She could almost feel his voice quivering and wanted some way to comfort him. Her body took control and she closed the gap giving him a small soft kiss.

"You'll never let me down," she said and walked away. Braylen stood there stunned with a grin on his face. She had managed to answer a few questions in those few seconds. He relived the moment over and over again as he watched her walk to the concession stand where their parents were already waiting. Braylen forced himself into the locker room as she disappeared from view.

Braylen managed to get dressed and walked out onto the field with his teammates. He watched the scoreboard click off the time until the game. He had fifty-four minutes until he met the beginning of his destiny. He stopped on the sideline and took a three hundred and sixty degree scan of his surroundings. He felt everybody that he had met in his entire life was perched in front of him now. He spotted Steph sitting with his mothers and grandparents. Frank and Dan were missing, but were easily found leaning up against the fence. Of course, he knew Pap Pap would want to scout the game before it even began. The waves of the warm up music met his ears and he gave one final glance at Steph to catch her smiling in his direction before he stepped out onto the fresh cut field. He felt alive, more alive than he had ever been in his whole life, as he went through the drills. His touches were spot on and as he looked around between the drills he felt a sense of being superhuman. The same feeling his father had shared eighteen years ago at his own state championship.

Warm up was over nearly as quick as it had began and Braylen felt as if time had just switched sides on him now. He felt it was hard to focus on what his coach was saying as all the excitement coursed through his veins. He stared around at his teammates that had grown to be family and could hear the bass of the music blaring outside. Inside his head, images of the thousands of people sitting outside began to cycle like a slideshow. He visualized everything that he felt would happen that day. Images of scoring, and holding that state championship trophy above his head appeared as real as if he could reach out and grab them. He knew that this was his moment, *the* moment where he would choose to be great or just fall to the legacy. The coach gave the final statement, "Boys, it's just you out on that field. It's now or never, this is your moment. Take it and run with it or you fall. I can't help you out there. It's your turn to show this town. You have family, friends, recruiters, and the whole damn state watching you in these next ninety minutes. It's your turn to be great, your turn to show everyone what this team is made of." Every word sank in deep for the team and they grabbed hands and prayed before they stepped back onto that field.

The team stepped out of that locker room and a wave of excitement hit them all. Braylen felt his stomach jump into his throat as he looked around. The first eleven starters shed their warm ups and waited while the announcers called out the visitors starting lineup. Each starter ran and shook the other team's hands. It was now onto the home team and Braylen heard his name and number called. His legs still felt cemented to the ground as he jogged over and shook the opposing team's hands, making sure to look the goalie in the eyes and joined his team out on the center of the pitch. He looked around at the fans cheering his name and felt as if he had never even been on that very field before. The cameras staged behind the goals, the reporters, the fans; it was all surreal. The cameras flashed, people screamed, and the screams somehow morphed into Braylen and his ten teammates huddled in the middle of the field. Braylen felt the need to say a few last words before the game started.

"Guys, as coach said, this is it! We leave nothing on this field tonight! I don't care if we all have to be carted off in ambulances from exhaustion or broken bones, we are going to win this game! We have to win this game for each other, and for this town, and for my father, watching down on us. For all our families, these ninety minutes decide what we will tell our grandchildren decades from now. Let's fucking do it, boys! Time to be heroes!"

The game started and it seemed, instantly, all his surroundings beyond that playing field vanished. It also seemed as if the playing level had instantly risen. He had never been placed on the ground more by any defense put together than those backs had done in the first five minutes. With every touch, Braylen was granted zero room to breathe or to become any type of playmaker. It had started out as a largely defensive and physical game, but the Christian County's defense had come to play as well. The referees were letting the game go on as it should and granted very few calls that the strikers begged for every time they were muscled off the ball. Braylen could tell this game was going to be harder to win than he could have ever imagined. He dribbled the ball granting himself space with only minutes left in the first half and booted the ball towards the bottom opposite corner of the goalie's postition. It was a shot that had never failed him before and was sure to go in.

At the last moment, the goalie managed to get his outstretched glove on the ball enough to make it kiss off the post and out of bounds. The excitement that had burst inside Braylen as he watched the shot was transformed into disappointment only seconds later. It was enough to take the wind out of anyone's sails and Braylen fully understood why he would be seeing that goalie in the future as he moved on to the next level. The corner kick was granted to the home team and the visiting team's monstrous defenders pushed it out without little trouble. Their midfielder traveled with the ball just over half field and the referee blew his whistle for half time. It was the longest forty-five minutes Braylen had experienced in his life. He wiped the sweat from his face and ran to join his team in the locker room for the fifteen minute half.

The coach only granted the team a select few words before the second half. "Work the sidelines, you will turn those defenders eventually and get your damn laces or some part of your body on that ball and eventually it will go in. Forty-five minutes guys, that's not too much to ask is it?" The team gave the desired unified "NO" and placed their hands in the circle to run out on the field. Frank and Dan tried to stop Braylen for a pep talk before he made it out onto the field.

"I know, the sidelines," Braylen brushed them off with a smile.

"You know, gorillas like bananas," Frank answered making sense to no one but Braylen. The teenager rejoined his team taking a hand full of shots and stealing glances at the sidelines. He saw his mother, Kareen, Steph, and his grandparents all staring down on him. He knew that in the next forty-five minutes he carried all their hopes and dreams.

"Yeah. Gorillas like bananas," he whispered to himself and laughed under his breath as he got in position to start the second half.

The second half started out nearly identical to the first half, but both teams had managed to place more shots on goal as every defense, no matter what the skill level, is apt to break down at least a handful of times in a game. Braylen was still closely guarded, but noticed that they had not shown so much respect towards the capabilities of his counterpart. Braylen knew that his fellow forward would be able to handle the task. Winning that state championship would be based on what the score at the end of the game was, not individual performances. Braylen began feeding his teammate the ball as soon as he received it instead of taking the touches he had taken his entire life to create space and get a shot. This seemed to baffle the opposing team and actually opened up more space for the forwards. Braylen and his teammate were between midfield and the eighteen yard box, when Braylen received the ball. He then chipped it over his defender's head and in front of his teammate. It was a perfect one-on-one opportunity just inside the box and his teammate was sure to score. The striker placed the ball in the lower right corner of the net and the crowd erupted.

The wind was taken instantly back out of their sails, however, as the sideline referee stood cemented just before the eighteen, his flag lowered parallel to the ground signaling for offsides. The crowd was reduced to a low murmur and the scoreboard switched back to the zero zero. The defender booted the ball away from the place kick. It felt as if it was a day that absolutely nothing was going to go right for the home team. The opposing team started gaining more and more advantages and shots on goal, but as he had for the whole tournament that Christian County goalie had risen to the challenge. The game wound down and Braylen couldn't help but think he was going to have to rely on his teammate in a penalty kick shootout to decide just who the state champions would be. Braylen watched as the clocked ticked down to zeros across the board and wondered how much stoppage time the referee would grant the crowd before giving in to penalty kicks.

The stopper on his team snatched Braylen's attention away from the scoreboard as he executed a perfect slide tackle through one of the opposing teams forwards. The defender then carried the ball to midfield and placed it to the sideline where a wing was eagerly waiting. The wing carried it down to about the eighteen and handed the ball off to Braylen who was on the right corner of the eighteen. Braylen took a touch with a defender and a goalie directly in front of him. Everything disappeared except for the ball, that goalie, and the goal directly behind him as Braylen was able to catch the defender off balance. Braylen looked down at the ball and back up at the goalie knowing he had to pull the trigger.

"Gorillas love bananas," he whispered to himself as he placed the outside of his cleat on the inside of the ball. The goalie guessed the direction of the ball correctly and instantly dove opposite corner to save what a normal textbook shot would be. The goalie had not taken into account, however, where Braylen had placed his cleat on the ball when he kicked it.

The ball curved outward to near post and rested inside the goal. Braylen had performed what even most professionals were not able to: a "Banana kick" that causes the ball to curve outwards instead of inwards. Braylen fell to the ground encompassing what had just taken place. What his once washed up grandfather had instructed was now his ticket to a state championship goal. He picked himself up to his knees and couldn't fight the emotion as his teammates pulled him the rest of the way up with the opposite teams goalie laying crushed on the ground just yards in front of him. Everything that had happened the previous ninety minutes had now disappeared as he watched the scoreboard click from zero to one. A few moments later, the referee granted an end to the suspense and blew the whistle for full time. They had won the state championship.

The home team's fans and reserves stormed the field while the opposite team lay crushed on the ground. Braylen jogged over to the opposing team's goalie, who sat rested against a goalpost.

"I'll be seeing you soon," Braylen said with a smile as he patted the crushed teenager on the back.

"Yeah . . . yeah, you will," The goalie forced a smile and an answer as tears streamed down his face. The mob then encompassed Braylen, his team lifting him in the air. Up on their shoulders he felt like he was the king of the world. No one's thinking about my father now, he thought to himself as he watched the commotion. Steph ran up to him and his teammates placed him back on level ground so they could talk. There was no talking, however, as he could see her eyes were welled with tears of excitement. He wrapped his arms around the girl and gave her a deep kiss in front of the thousands of people, neither one having a care in the world what anyone thought. The smile on her face grew larger and Braylen was now greeted by his mother. Heather gave him a bone crushing hug and kissed her son on the forehead.

"You beat that legacy," she whispered into his ear and then let him join his team to receive their hardware and deal with reporters.

* * *

Braylen awoke the next morning to the feeling of his sheets moving. He had only slept four hours from all the excitement that had been had the night before. The team had met at his mother's diner after the game and tables were moved around to have a press conference sort of setup for the media. He rubbed his eyes as he felt he smelled fresh breakfast being placed on his nightstand. Steph sat on the bed and placed her hand on his leg.

"Yes, it's all real," she said with a smile and gave him a kiss as Braylen forced his eyes open. She then handed him the weekly paper still wrapped in plastic. "This came and we figured you would want to be the first one to read it." Braylen kissed his love again and opened up the paper. At first glance it had a picture of him winding up to kick the ball and another picture beside it showing the ball as it crossed the goal line into the net. Below it, he read the article, picking out one more picture at the bottom. The article talked of the intensity of the game and how Braylen had lived up to a legacy; a legacy left by his father. The article went on to explain the legacy of Landon Maston that had been left behind for Braylen.

The third picture, the one that caught Braylen's attention, was not happy, however, and was small. It showed what appeared to be his mother's store with caution tape over the door. Below it read a small excerpt, "Just under 18 years ago, Landon Maston was gunned down by an out of towner, Jason Thomas, leaving behind a legacy for our hero to carry."

Braylen looked at it for a second and then at Steph. "Jason Thomas?" he began, "Isn't that your father?"

Made in the USA  
Lexington, KY  
28 August 2014